HAWK'S HEART
Guardians of the Fae Realms: Book 4
JL Madore

Hawk's Heart: Guardians of the Fae Realms

JL Madore -- 1st ed.

ISBN: 978-1-998372-61-4

CHAPTER ONE

Hawk

There's this incredible moment during sex when the tip of a male's cock breaches the opening of his mate and then glides forward with a moist rush of pleasure. The fucking that follows is great too, but that singular moment never fails to steal my breath. I've experienced it while having sex with women and fae females for decades. Whether in their pussy, mouth, or ass, it was that same breath-stopping pleasure.

Breach... Thrust... And glide into succulent pleasure.

What I never expected was how good it would feel to be the one on the receiving end of a male's cock. Hand to goddess, when Jaxx's cock pushes past the constriction of my ass and glides inside me... I swear my heart stops.

There's this moment of suspended time when everything in me shudders and I surrender with such succulence I am momentarily lost.

I've learned this is perfectly alright.

Nothing bad happens when I give up control. Jaxx doesn't

take advantage or make me feel weak or diminished for wanting to be dominated. If anything, I feel stronger.

I never expected giving up control would make me feel powerful. But it does—*he* does.

Jaxx fucks like an Olympic champion. And every spare moment that I'm not caught up in the drama and chaos of my roles of alpha mate, CEO of the Fae Concealment Organization, or investigator of whatever the fuckety-fuck is going on with the Black Knight and his crusade to frame me for crimes against my people, I'm obsessing about how and when he'll fuck me next.

It's distracting... but it's the most erotic distraction I've ever had the pleasure of experiencing. Shit. That sounds bad.

Without a doubt, I'm totally, erotically distracted by Calli too... it's just different.

With Jaxx, it's... rougher, edgier. Raw.

Calli is a scorching hot need and I hunger to be inside her for my sanity and to keep my heart throbbing.

Jaxx keeps another organ of mine throbbing... and yeah, I'm so fucking into it, I've lost perspective.

"You good, hotness?"

The concern in Jaxx's tone snaps me out of my sexual revelations and brings me back to the point of my distraction. He has me right where both of us want me, bent over the rise of the bondage couch with my knees locked open and my hands strapped down. "Yeah, perfect. I got lost in my dirty mind anticipating. Carry on."

The sexy chuckle behind me has my cock twitching. "As long as you're good."

"One hundy percent. My only problem is that you're not fucking me yet."

There's that chuckle again.

Jaxx is standing between the knee platforms, his thighs brushing the backs of mine as he drizzles heated oil on my back.

With torturous care, he massages his way from my shoulder blades down to my ass crack. "So impatient, avian. Doesn't your cock feel good in that trough?"

I pump against the silicone milking sleeve in the center of the vinyl cushion and swallow. He set the suction tight and when I move, it's like my cock is being gripped for a rough rub and tug. "Yeah, it's good."

"But not what you're jonesin' for?"

"Not even close." His hands are amazing, his fingers strong. He's been reading up on sensual massage and Kama Sutra. It's really, fucking paying off.

I close my eyes and try to breathe, reminding myself that *he's* in charge. I surrendered control.

"Make a wish. Tell me what you want."

"Your cock, my ass. Now."

He chuckles, pulling the slide of the oil down to toy with the rim of my ass. "You are wound up tonight."

"It's been too long since Vancouver."

"Agreed." His slick thumb breaches the tight knot of flesh. I shudder, the warmth of pre-cum leaking into the sheath. I try not to pump my hips forward. I don't want to be a chump and pump off before the action even gets started. "Do you want sexy slow or the bite of burn?"

I groan, my heart pounding at the base of my throat. "Burn. Hard and fast. Fuck me."

After the heat of the oil, the lube is cold. The contrast is delicious. More thumb-fucking and then his engorged crown plays in place.

"You are sexy as fuck, you know that, right?"

The hand restraints clink as I pull back. I need him inside me to the point of me going feral. I want this more than I can make sense of. "Jaxx. Do you want me to beg? I'm losing my mind here."

"No beggin' necessary. If I wasn't in the same position, I'd draw this out and torture you more. I'll get to that later. First, I think I'll fuck you senseless."

Yes. That.

He thrusts his hips forward and penetrates me hard and fast. We both let off a throaty groan and I drop my forehead against the padded headrest. It's perfect. I asked for bite and burn and he delivered.

The invasion isn't gentle and the sharp twinge of pain from forcing my body to accept his cock is perfect.

He pauses for a second as we both settle and then grips my hips. "The safeword?"

"Hydrogen."

Jaxx chuckles. "The most combustible element."

"The kid's not wrong. We've come close to combusting a few times."

Jaxx unlocks his hips, withdraws a couple of inches, and slams home. The penetration is deep, and I push my forehead into the pad and brace myself.

"Test my limits, jaguar. No boundaries. If it enters your mind, I'm game to try it. I'm all yours."

Jaxx

Hawk's too fucking much. Harnessed and trussed to this red vinyl fuck bench, he's locked down tight. I'm totally getting off on the rush of power. Focusing on pleasuring him, I build momentum until I'm pounding home and my lungs burn with the exertion. My jaguar roars in my head and I smile. Yeah, buddy, we can do this all night long.

And Hawk can take it.

Vancouver was eye-opening for both of us. During that side-trip to the Great White North, I learned as much about myself as I did about our billionaire corporate raider. One of my favorite self-discoveries is that my dominant side loves getting rough with him.

I've never been much of a power player behind closed doors before, but with Hawk, I want his submission. If he needs to hold the reins in public, that's cool.

'Cause right here... with him locked down and me hitting him hard and deep, I'm a fucking god.

No boundaries. I know what a momentous statement that is for him and I'll reward his faith in me.

He's too sexy. He's as tall as Brant but has a lean and muscled frame like a runner instead of the mass of bulk and strength like our Bear. And unlike the subtle and supple beauty of Kotah's body, Hawk's tats and piercings set the stage for one helluva tough and edgy male.

He doesn't disappoint on that front.

I never knew I was into the haunted bad boy type, but hells to the yeah—I *soooo* am.

Sweat drips from my brow and I grab the hand towel I set out for just this reason. Fucking Hawk is an all-in, full-bodied, cardio event.

I learned that in Vancouver a couple of weeks go.

He's addictive and tireless. And yeah, Kotah's right—together we are highly combustible.

In and out... In and out.

The air is filled with the sounds of sex, moist flesh slapping, the bench feet inching across the floor, his throaty gasps blend with my breathy ones. Hawk's arms are flexed tight, his grip on the hand pads of the bench clenched and white-knuckled. He's pushing back each time my pelvis hits his ass and I know he's getting close because his breathing starts to catch.

I learned that sound over hours spent together.

It never fails to crank me up.

Leaning sideways, I drop the towel on the little table where I have my oil and lube supplies and grab the little black remote.

"I'm ampin' things up, my man. Hold off. I don't want you comin' yet."

Without losing my rhythm, I turn on the vibrator option on the cock sleeve that's milking him.

"Oh, fuck," Hawk shudders like he's being electrocuted, and his hips spasm until he regains control.

"Good?"

"So good," he gasps, dropping his head forward. "I'm not going to last."

I turn off the vibrator and stop pumping. "Sorry? What's that now?"

Hawk groans. "Dammit, don't stop."

"Are you gonna blow?"

"No," he shouts. "I won't... I swear."

I reward his declaration by adding a round of friction lube and resuming my in and out. The lube warms up almost instantly and I have to focus or *I'm* going to be the one losing it. When I get the tingling in my balls locked down, I turn the vibrator back on low. "You good?"

"Yeah."

"You want more?"

"Yeah."

"You gonna lose it?"

"Not until you say so."

"Good man."

I turn up the vibrator and though he shudders again, he doesn't convulse as wildly. With a flick of my thumb, I slide the tension dial and tighten the grip of the silicon sheath milking his cock with each forward thrust of my hips.

Hawk locks his elbows and starts to pant, pushing back in a hot frenzy. His fingers grip and regrip the hand pads and I smile at his distress. "You want to come bad, don't you?"

"Yeah... so bad."

"But you won't." He shakes his head and sweat drips off his brow.

"Who's yer daddy?"

He barks out a laugh. "You are."

"Yeah?"

"Yeah," he gasps, his arms trembling with the force of his grip.

Turning up the remote another notch, I smile as I feel the vibration tingle against my cock from the inside. Man, I could torture him all night long and I bet he'd hold out. He's been the dom so many years, he knows how the game is played. I love that he's this determined to give me what I want.

Deciding to put him out of his misery, I drop the remote onto the table and grab his hips with both hands. "Okay, Hawk, let's do this. We're goin' hard. Take as much as you can and then show me how good you feel. Lose your mind."

The next few minutes is an ode to slapping flesh and breathless grunts. The two of us are all sweat and sex and carnal pleasures. There's nothing in this world but the two of us.

And then, his head comes back, and he thrusts his cock hard against the couch. The locking of his body clenches my cock so tight, I can't hold off.

Too. Fucking. Sexy.

I thrust hard and join him in the release of a lifetime—my lifetime anyway. Hot jets of cream mark his insides and my cat lets loose. The rolling purr of my jaguar brings on another wave of Hawk gasping out obscenities.

I love his filthy mouth. It gets worse the better he gets off. By that scale, that orgasm rocked his world. After he's thoroughly marked as mine, I collapse onto his sweaty back.

Reaching around, I grip the arm braces to keep from crushing him. His chest is heaving almost as hard as mine as I blanket him with my body. Before I release the restraints wrapped around his wrists and knees, I nuzzle the back of his neck and nip his nape. "Good start. You up for a few more hours of that?"

Hawk surprises me by turning his head and offering his mouth. "I'm up for a lifetime of that, Jaguar."

"Good answer." With that, I release his restraints and pull out. Taking off the condom I wore for anal, I drop it into the garbage and help him off the sex couch. He's a little stiff, so I escort him to the bed in our Den of Debauchery—as Kotah so aptly named it—and get him settled.

After a quick trip to my supply table, I move everything to the king-sized bed. Hawk watches me, his sated smile far too sexy. "Got somethin' on your mind, mate of mine?"

"Mutual cock sucking," he says.

I climb up to join him. "Done deal. I like how you think. Top or bottom?"

Hawk snorts and rolls onto his back. "I've got nothing left in my arms and legs right now. Assume the position, Jaguar. Swing around and give me something to suck on."

I chuckle and swing around. "Work. Work. Work."

CHAPTER TWO

Calli

Talk about distracting. Kotah and I are sitting through yet another Fae Prime training session and trying to care what his mother is blathering on about. The only thing on my mind is stripping down and mounting my mates. The mating bond connecting the five of us is working overtime and oh my good gods, whatever Hawk and Jaxx are playing at is twanging every lusty chord of need I've got.

I cast a sideways glance at Kotah and yeah, my wolf's not doing much better. He's biting his bottom lip and running his hands over his thighs so much I wouldn't be surprised if his pants are threadbare underneath.

"And, if the Council should ever need to call an emergency summit—" Yadda, yadda, yadda.

My cell vibrates in my lap and I check the message. It's from Brant. *Holy fuck. Where are you and the wolf? My arm is getting tired.*

I snort and meet the Prima's disapproving glare. "Something funny, Calliope?"

"Sorry, Prima. Kotah and I are needed elsewhere. We'll have to pick this up again at a later date."

"Excuse me?"

I hand Kotah my phone and he reads the text. Maybe he prepared himself better not to laugh than I did, or maybe he's simply better at playing the part of compliant pawn, but his facial expression gives nothing away. "Apologies, Mother. Calli is right. This needs to be addressed immediately."

"What does? Where are you two running off to?"

"Urgent mate business. Let Keyla know when you're available tomorrow and we'll try to reconvene. Excuse us."

Kotah takes my hand and helps me to my feet. We're out of the royal wing and practically jogging back to the Timber Trails Suite in the next minute.

I glance down to ensure my nipples aren't poking out the front of my shirt and sigh. "Good gawd, we need to coordinate meetings and sextathalons better. I'm so wet and keyed up I shouldn't be near any wildlings right now. You guys and your stupid heightened sense of smell. I'm a walking billboard for hot and horny."

Kotah barks out a laugh, gesturing with a wave of his hand for the people in the corridor to move out of our way. Sometimes it pays to be married to the next Fae Prime... like when you want to bypass congestion in the halls of the royal palace to get home and have sex.

"Luckily, being the only phoenix in existence, no one has any frame of reference. They don't know the cues of your scents like your four mates do."

"Seriously?"

He nods. "Seriously. Unless you let them know you're horny while you smell like this, they won't know."

"Unless they put together the fact that *you're* horny when I smell like this."

"Well, yes. There certainly is that to consider. So there, you're not the billboard for hot and horny. *We* are."

We reach the private staircase that leads to our home away from home and tackle those steps two at a time. If nothing else, my daily training is starting to pay off.

I may not be strong enough to fly without a spectacular crash and burn, but I can run a set of stairs like Rocky if it means I get to the sex part faster.

"There you are," Maggie Stanton says, beaming at us as we crest the top landing.

She and Jonathan are coming down the corridor looking adorable, as always. The Texan jaguars are tanned and blonde and move with the same stalking sway as their jungle cats do. There's no knowing them and not loving them. As Brant says... they're good people.

"We stopped by your suite just now to drop off this. Three fae species could do what you think your friend Riley has done. If you have time to go through it now—"

"No. I'm good," I say, with far too much vigor.

Jaxx's mother arches a brow.

I scrub a hand over my face and rake my hair out of my face. "Sorry, Mama... we're just..."

"Headed for some private mate time," Kotah says.

Maggie sets the file in my hand and smiles. "You don't have to apologize or explain to us."

My cheeks flush hot and I roll my eyes, sending Kotah a stink-eyed glare.

He bursts out laughing. "What? They knew without me saying anything."

"You said no one would know."

"Mama and Daddy are around us enough to recognize the scent. I swear to you the whole palace doesn't know."

Maggie shakes her head. "Goddess no. And don't be embarrassed. We'll talk tomorrow, kids. Off you go. Love you."

"Love you." Kotah kisses Mama's cheek, tugs me back into motion, and we close the distance between us and our naked mates.

By the time my sweet prince places his hand on the security panel outside the door of our suite, my heart is racing. I'm waiting for the scanner to grant us access, but before it has time, the door flies open and Brant yanks me inside.

There's no need for any preamble as he pulls me into his arms and crushes me against his broad chest. He can smell my need and he's naked and hard against my crotch.

His lips are rough on mine, but I'll never complain.

I love it when my guys are out of their minds and out of control. He pins me up against the wall and my feet are almost a foot off the ground.

"Hey, Bear." Kotah closes the door and locks it behind us. "Can I make myself useful and relieve Calli of her underthings?"

Brant grunts and pulls his hips back far enough for Kotah to gain access to me from below. My shoes are the first to go, then warm hands skim up the tender flesh of my inner thighs to grab hold of the flimsy strip of silk keeping the three of us from where we want to be so bad.

When that's taken care of, my cotton sheath dress is pushed up to my waist and I wrap my legs around the thick and muscled trunk of my bear's hips.

The head of his cock prods at my core but he doesn't push in. I shake my head at the hesitation, knowing what holds him back. He's huge and doesn't like to take me without a few orgasms and playtime first.

He worries about being too much and splitting me.

Yes, it happens, but I've explained to him that the invasive fullness of him doesn't bother me in the slightest. In fact, it's the opposite. The pleasure-pain of him driving inside me is erotic as hell.

I wrap my heels around his ass and pull him inside. Once the

12

penetration starts, I throw my head back and cry out. The sheer satisfaction of having him pulsing and prodding inside me is worth any momentary discomfort.

Besides, I'm a phoenix. I have miraculous healing.

"Fuck, I needed you, Beautiful," Brant grunts, crushing me between his massive frame and the wall at my back.

"Me too." My eyes roll back as I close them and I let the world slip away. Brant starts a slow and steady rhythm of invade and retreat, and my body tingles to life. My phoenix grows stronger and more aware every day.

And right now, she's lighting me up inside.

"We both do." Kotah's naked now and I feel bad that for a moment, I forgot about my wolf's pleasure. I reach for him and he takes my hand.

He kisses my palm and sets my hand on Brant's muscled shoulder. "Let Brant take what he needs, *Chigua*. I'll enjoy the show and can take care of things myself for a bit."

That doesn't seem to fly with Brant. He pulls me off the wall and heads for the stairs. In a normal, human relationship, a girl might wonder if her man can carry her up a flight of stairs to the bedroom joined while gripping the back of her head and kissing the ever-loving breath out of her.

I don't have to worry.

Brant is as strong as the bear who lives within him.

When we get to the bedroom, he stops at the end of the bed, lays me back on the mattress, and stays standing.

Hooking his arms under my knees, he lifts my legs and starts a slow and torturous ride. Kotah climbs onto the bed with me and I reach between his legs.

One thing I've made really clear—I love sucking cock.

At first, they were all, *'Oh, no. You don't have to.'* They've learned not to argue. It isn't an obligation for me, it's a turn on. As much as having them make love to me, or fuck me, or service me with their tongues, mouths, and toys.

Kotah crawls across the bed and I guide his erection into my mouth. My wolf has a scent to his skin that is uniquely his own. Where Jaxx smells like fresh air and spruce trees, Kotah's skin smells like earth and wilderness.

It's addictive.

I grip him against the base of his cock and take him deep into my mouth. After sucking and giving him his welcome. I pull back a little and flick my tongue through the beads of precum leaking from his tip.

Kotah's hips quiver. He's holding back his urge to pump into my mouth. My sweet prince. Always a gentleman. Growling, I get more aggressive and let my teeth score the heated flesh. I've always loved how responsive his body is to my desire.

While I'm getting my groove on with Kotah's cock, Brant finds my clit and is rubbing the fleshy pad of his thumb over my exposed nerves as he continues to fill me with the ecstasy I only feel with one of my mates inside me.

My orgasm builds as a hot pang, low in my groin. I grind against Brant, coaxing it, fanning it from a smolder until it's ready to ignite.

"So, fucking beautiful," Brant says, his voice husky and low. "I could come just by watching you get off."

Kotah, chuckles. "You have. Many times."

"Oh, yeah. Right you are, Wolf. Right you are."

"More, Bear," I gasp, wriggling against him. I want the twinge of the stretch I get when he drives hard. "Make me ache."

"You don't have to ask twice." Brant's pace doubles and he presses my legs back. With my shins against his shoulders and my ankles above his head, he gets serious.

I grunt as his fingers grip harder and he's hammering me in earnest. "Yes... that."

"Your wish is my deepest pleasure, mate. I can take you like this all week long."

I have no doubt. Just thinking about that brings on a wave of keening. My inner muscles clench and then I explode.

Kotah's mouth is on my nipples.

Oh, I lost track of him moving.

Too swept away to try to figure it out, I ride the waves of my release with one of his hands tweaking the tight tip of my breast and him suckling and licking and nipping the other.

My hips buck but Brant never loses his hold on me. He's a machine and I'm so thankful for his skills. As I come down from the rolling waves pulsing through me, he climbs onto the bed and with one arm around my back, moves me up to the pillows.

He hasn't lost it yet and honestly, it wouldn't slow him down much if he had. The refractory time for wildling males is next to nothing. I'm a truly blessed woman.

Rolling me onto his broad, muscled chest, Brant smacks my ass and chuckles when I yelp. "Okay, I'm just messing with you. Now that I've taken the edge off and am in better control, how about I make love to my mates?"

I give Kotah a look. "What do you say, sweet prince? Should we let our bear have his way with us?"

Kotah's smile is the balm to my soul. "He has my vote. But speak for yourself on the taking the edge off part, Bear. My wolf is still pacing."

I roll off Brant and open my arms. "Then we've got work to do. Good thing we have all night."

Jaxx

I wake dazed and with my jaguar prowling within. It takes a moment for my senses to catch up with reality. It's the scent of Hawk on my skin that gets me there. *Right*, the two of us are in the Den of Debauchery. The groan in the darkness has me rolling over to check the bed beside me. Hawk is twitching, his legs kicking, his unconscious struggles coming out in broken groans.

"Hey, Hawk? You okay?"

His eyes flick open and he grabs me and flips me on my back faster than I would've thought possible. Maybe it's because he's my mate and my guard was down or maybe he's that good, I have no clue.

Either way, the result is the same.

There's a six-foot-four, alpha male straddling my hips with his hands wrapped around my throat.

Quick thinking in a crisis is a strength of mine and one of the reasons I joined the First Responders team of the FCO. I don't panic. Instead, I bring my arm up between his wrists, lock my grip on my other hand, and use leverage to break his hold on my windpipe.

The moment I'm free from his grip, I turn the tables and flip him so I'm straddling his hips and have his wrists pinned to the mattress.

Leaning down, I try to find my mate and lover in those haunted, steel-gray eyes. "Hawk. It's me. It's Jaxx. Where are you right now?"

His gaze is vacant and he's fighting my hold. Unlike when this happened with Calli, I'm not an unprepared female and I'm not afraid. I understand he has violent episodes and he's not in control. This isn't him.

This is something bubbling up from his subconscious.

As much as I want to hug it out, I can't let go of his wrists or he'll hurt me or himself. With little else to do but keep trying to snap him out of it, I lean into my hold on him and kiss him. "It's me, tough guy. Hydrogen. You need to stop. That's our safe-word. Do you remember?"

I kiss him more, trying to reach him, but I get nothing.

When Brant got through to him it was after he threw him

across the room and threatened to rip him to shreds. I can't do that. I won't. He's in there and I doubt violence will help him wherever he's struggling deep inside.

With that in mind, I reach deep inside myself and access our mating bond. My ties to my mates are evenly distributed between all four. Hawk's aren't. Hawk's are strongest with me and Calli. I need to use that to my advantage.

"Come on, hotness. It's me. Your jaguar."

I kiss him roughly, biting his lip hard enough to draw blood. His pupils flare and if this wasn't such a fucking shit show I'd laugh. Seriously? After all the sex and in the middle of a mental meltdown, me biting him turns his crank?

He's still fighting my hold, but not as frantically. I kiss him again, teasing the spot on his lip I injured, my cat excited at the taste of blood. Instead of fighting to get away from my mouth, this time his lips respond and my heart slows from a frantic thunder to erratically elevated.

"That's it." I lick the blood, my cat letting off a long, languid purr. "Snap out of it. Leave whatever darkness you're in and come back to me. Hydrogen."

I know the split-second my message gets through. Hawk's entire body goes rigid beneath me and his breath locks in his chest.

"Everything is fine." I allow my purr to rumble on. "I'm here, Hawk. I've got you. You're safe. We're good. Everythin' is fine."

"Fuck me... I did it again, didn't I?"

"You did nothin' but get your ass kicked by your jaguar dom. I've got you. It's my job to keep you safe when we're in here like this, yeah?"

I smell the rush of emotion and I ease up on the vise-grip of his wrists. Rolling us both to the side, I pull his chest to mine and toss the sheet over us. "I've got you. Wherever you were just then, let that shit go. You're safe here with me."

After a few minutes of me hugging a stiff and reluctant

participant, he relaxes in my arms and nuzzles into my neck. "Let me breathe you in for a bit."

I smile and caress gentle circuits up and down his back from the nape of his neck to his tailbone and back again. "You do whatever you need to do. Release the bad juju. I'm here. I've got you, Hawk."

He shakes his head against my collarbone. "Could you not call me that? Hawk is a name I took on to stay hard and distant. Whatever's broken inside me it's from a lifetime of being hard and distant. My mother always called me Bastian. Would you mind? I think… it would help."

"Whatever you need, Bastian." I draw a shuddered breath as another of his walls crumbles. I need to keep him talking. I have enough trauma counseling training that I know I can help him. "Your mother… you've never mentioned her before. Tell me about her. What was she like?"

He stiffens a bit but I don't let him pull away.

"I've got you, remember? Trust me with what's broken inside you. I'm a paramedic. I scoop up roadkill and patch people back together for a livin'."

He chuffs, his breath warm against my neck. "And you think talking about my mother is the key? That's a little on the nose Freudian, don't you think?"

I chuckle. "I'm not suggestin' you have an Oedipus complex, simply that I'd like to hear about the woman who knew a softer side of you. You've told us a dozen times about how hard and manipulative your father was, but you've never mentioned your mother until now."

He lays quiet for a while and I listen to his breathing. Whether he opens up or not isn't a huge deal. Whatever he's sorting through in his head is much-needed housekeeping and he's doing it with my arms around him.

S'all good.

After a long while, he draws a deep breath. "Her name was

Elizaveta, though her close friends called her Liza. She was tall and demure, and had long, chestnut hair that shone gold in the sunlight."

"She sounds lovely."

"She was. Before she met and married my father, she ran a chain of occult shops. I remember... she loved to work with essential oils, so she always smelled wonderful."

"And she called you Bastian?"

He nods. "My father hated the informality of it. To him, I was always Sabastian or boy... He used that a lot. Boy, get your ass in here. Boy, what's this I hear from your instructor? With her, things were softer... sweeter."

"That's good. I'm glad you had someone who loved you. Even if it wasn't for long enough."

"Yeah. I've often wondered how I would've turned out if I'd been seventeen instead of seven when she died."

"Likely very different. I can't imagine losin' Mama so young. It must've been a sad time."

He nods. "For a long time, I wondered if my father loved her or if he simply acquired her like he did so many treasures in his life. It was hard to tell with him. I think having me was her idea. When she was gone, he didn't know what to do with me. I kinda just became one of his possessions."

"That's sad. I'm sorry you grew up feelin' like you didn't matter. That's shitty."

He shrugs. "He'd always been more interested in business than us, so when she was gone, he wasn't prepared to deal with a sad little boy. He pushed harder at work and he also pushed harder at home."

"Did he hurt you?" I'm hesitant to ask, but I'd like to know what I'm dealing with and how big the hurdles are ahead of us. "You don't have to tell me anythin' you're not ready to share, but it would help if—"

"Not in the way you mean. No. Being broken and unapproachable has nothing to do with any kind of sexual or physical abuse."

Thank fuck. "I'm not gonna lie. I'm really freakin' glad to hear it. I'd hate to have to fly to London to track down and kill a powerful billionaire who hurt you in another lifetime."

He leans back and when he meets my gaze, I can tell he's gauging how serious I am.

"I'd be on a plane in the mornin'."

His smile warms the cold place in the pit of my belly. "There's no need, but thank you."

I roll onto my side and adjust the pillow we're sharing. Our faces are inches apart and with our voices low, it feels like we can share any secret. "So, the violent episodes aren't physical or sexual abuse. Do you think they stem from psychological abuse?"

He nods. "Very likely. My father doesn't do anything halfway. When he fucked me up and tore me down, he did it with more power and panache than anyone else could. And then, he convinced me it was my fault. It's crazy what you believe as a kid. I knew he was driven and cold, but it took me years to realize the damage he was doing to me."

I brush my fingers over the flexing tension in his jaw and lean in for a kiss. "You're the stronger man. You broke away and remade yourself with no help from him."

Hawk chuckles. "Well, no *willing* help from him. I did grab two-hundred grand from the library safe the day I left. I may have been determined to leave him and that life behind but I wasn't stupid."

I laugh and the tension in my chest eases.

Hawk's come a long way from the arrogant prick who wanted to sever our connections and deny the guardianship. "I —for one—am proud of you. And I think your mother would be too."

He doesn't look so sure, but hey, baby steps. First, we'll

release the toxic energy, and then, we'll change the tapes that run through his head. I touch the broken skin on his lip. "Sorry, I bit you."

He frowns and runs his fingers over my throat, looking for the damage he did. He didn't have me in his hold long, so I doubt there's even a mark. "Sorry, I tried to choke you."

I shrug. "Tried and failed miserably. Now, do you want to go back to sleep or snuggle some more?"

He rolls over toward the bedside table and grabs the wrist cuffs we used earlier. When he hands them to me, he shakes his head to cut off my objection. "I'm exhausted, but I won't sleep unless I know you're safe."

"You won't hurt me. I won't let you. You don't have—"

"Please, Jaxx. Do this for me. I want to be held but won't relax unless I'm sure you're safe."

My jaguar growls, but I give in and do as he asks. With his wrists bound together, I shift behind him, position my arm under his ear and the other over his ribs to hug him and spoon him tight to his ass.

"We're supposed to be sleeping here, Jaxx. No slipping me your pickle."

I nip the flesh of his shoulder blade and purr. "It didn't turn out so bad the last time, did it?"

His chuckle is deep and sexy as fuck. "It stands as one of the all-time highlights of my life. There are moments with you that I'm so overwhelmed I feel like Kotah's right and I might spontaneously combust."

"Me too. Hydrogen."

"Yeah. Hydrogen."

CHAPTER THREE

Kotah

I'm the first one to wake in the morning and leave Calli and Brant cuddled in bed to go start breakfast. I snag a pair of sweatpants off the dresser and pad barefoot out of the master bedroom. After easing the door shut, I cover things up and head downstairs.

I love that the design of our suite mirrors my home at Northwood. As a man, there are moments I forget I'm trapped at the palace. My wolf never forgets. He's restless and paces and remains on edge. He doesn't let me sleep more than the four hours he needs to function.

It's irrelevant that I might need... or want more sleep. He hates being here. Hates that there's nowhere wild and green to run. Hates that everything about this place goes against what's important to us.

There's nothing to be done about that, so I might as well get up and make myself useful.

Puttering in the kitchen has become a new favorite pastime

of mine. Adahy stocks our fridge and cupboards. She makes us fresh pastries and dinners every other day. And leaves me recipe cards of things she knows I loved as a boy that I might like to try making for my mates.

She's never steered me wrong.

This morning, I'm making a steak and eggs breakfast casserole with mushrooms, sun-dried tomatoes, and in honor of Calli's love for Tater Tots, I'm adding those as well. Adahy wasn't keen on me bastardizing the recipe but honestly, I don't care if the addition ruins a childhood favorite.

Calli's face will light up when she realizes what I've done and that's all the incentive I need.

I oil the iron skillet and set it on medium to heat up. Next, I go to the fridge and the pantry, assembling the ingredients I need: onion, sun-dried tomato, mushrooms, eggs, milk, steak tips…

"You're up early." Hawk crosses the living room, dressed to impress in slacks and black button-down dress shirt. He's looking well-rested considering how late he and Jaxx were up. "Your wolf still upset about being here?"

"How'd you know?"

He lifts a shoulder and strides over to where his French Press and designer blends are set up. "Reading people is my thing. I'm an observer, remember?"

It's true. He's been able to read all of us since the beginning. So why is it he's so blind when it comes to me? I've done everything I can think of to catch his attention. I've made my feelings clear and still he holds me at arm's reach.

I grab the cooking spray and catch my wolf's growl before it lets loose. My animal side is frustrated and edgy.

There's nothing to be gained by starting a fight.

I spray the casserole dish and set it aside. The oil in the skillet is beading, so I toss in the onions, tomato, and mushrooms. "I take it by the early hour and the attire you're headed into the office for another day of video conferencing?"

"For the morning at least. My Director of Operations, Hunter Gable, is concerned about an uptick in lesser fae protests. There have been a couple of confrontations over the last month that involved exposure."

"I thought after the Monster Rights Conference, the tension with the lesser fae was alleviated."

"Pacified, maybe, but it doesn't seem to have stuck. So, we're putting out fires this morning and then, I'm hoping to have some time with my mates this afternoon."

"All four of us or just your real mates?" The venom lacing my words rings in the air. The moment I hear it, I want to take it back. My throat tightens and I swallow past the lump in my throat.

Hawk winces. "Excuse me? My real mates?"

"Calli and Jaxx. The mates you choose versus the mates you don't." My gaze is locked on the vegetables I'm pushing around in the skillet. The scent and sizzle filling my senses.

"What the fuck, Kotah?"

I wave the spoon wishing I could breathe past the growing pressure in my lungs. My wolf is raging and I'm having a hard time tethering my wild side. "Apologies, this is not the conversation you need to have before you put out the fires of the realm. My wolf is cranky and you're needed elsewhere."

"Cranky or not, this sounds like something we should be talking about sooner rather than later."

I push the veggies to the side and add in the steak tips. "Forget I said anything. I'm tired."

"I don't doubt you are, but a comment like that doesn't bubble up out of nowhere. You've been stewing."

I stop stirring and meet his gaze. "And why wouldn't I? I've made it clear how I feel. I told you what I want and you turn me down every time. Why aren't I enough for you?"

Hawk's eyes flare wide and he steps in close. He grabs my biceps and I want to back away and drop my gaze—he's an alpha and it's my omega nature to submit.

I can't breathe. I need to get outside and run.

I need air.

"You've got that backward, Wolf. You *are* enough. You're too much. You're the fucking Prime Prince. You came to this mating with a clean slate and a pure soul. I'm tainted and cynical. Calli, Jaxx, and Brant... they're better for you. The best way for me to show you I care is to step back."

"Bullshit." I bare my canines and snap. I pull back and break free from his hold, my wolf's growl rumbling low and threatening. "That's a cop-out and you know it."

I need out of here.

I round the island and he's there blocking my way. My wolf is pushing forward, snarling inside me. "Get away from me, Hawk. I'm losing my wolf."

I push at him and he grips my wrist.

"If I'm fucking things up this badly, you don't get to throw it in my face and then run and hide. Let's hear it—all of it— because sure as shit there's more."

"I can't breathe..." My head is spinning and my wolf is going feral. I pull for freedom but Hawk's stronger. "I need air... I can't..."

Hawk

My heart is thundering when Kotah's eyes roll back in his head and he drops like a rock. It's only because I have him by the wrists that I save him from crashing completely.

"Kotah? What's wrong?" I feel for his pulse and maybe I'm

freaking out, but I don't feel anything. *"Jaxx!* Jaxx, I need you! *Now!"*

With no idea what else to do, I start CPR. I'm counting time for hand presses and about to lean in for air when Jaxx runs out of the Den and sees me straddling Kotah on the floor.

Without missing a beat, he up-and-overs the railing and launches down to the main level like a jaguar in the jungle. He lands on the kitchen table in a crouch and pounces again to land on the floor next to me. "What happened?"

"The fuck if I know."

Jaxx's hands are taking inventory of Kotah as Calli screams from above and Brant tears out of the master bedroom on her heels.

"Hawk, focus. What did he say? Chest pain? Dizzy. Can't breathe—"

"Can't breathe… and he was losing control of his wolf."

Jaxx leans over his mouth. "Stop compressions for a sec." He blows and frowns. "Brant, the med bag is in the workout room closet. Get it."

"What's wrong?" Calli asks

"His pulse is weak and rapid. Labored breathing. I'm guessing anaphylaxis."

"Guessing?"

"What do you need?" Brant drops the bag and rips it open. The zipper has no chance of survival.

Jaxx grabs the epi-autoinjector and slams it into the kid's thigh. "Someone get me Doc."

Brant's out the door and running across the hall in two racing strides.

"What happened exactly?" Jaxx grabs a stethoscope out of the bag and presses the disc to his chest.

I'm trying to think. Fuck. Crisis is my jam but—

"Hawk! I need you to focus, hotness. What the fuck were the two of you doing?

I run a hand over my hair. "I was on coffee. He was grilling stuff at the stove. He sprayed a dish, oiled a pan, stirred some vegetables..."

"What did he say? Were his words slurred? Was he confused or disoriented?"

"He was snappy, aggressive, picking a fight."

"That doesn't sound like Kotah," Calli says.

"It wasn't like him at all. He said he was tired. His wolf snapped at me."

"Kotah!" Keyla rushes in with Doc, both of them half-dressed. "What happened?"

The moment his sister drops to the floor beside him, Kotah flips from man to wolf and we all edge back. He snaps and growls, his head low.

"Give him space." Jaxx raises his palms. "His wolf is in full-ascension and is not a happy camper."

"At least he's upright." I drop to my ass on the floor. "Let him be as wild and cranky as he wants. If he's living and breathing, nothing else matters at the moment."

Calli

Keyla goes wolf and Kotah accepts her being near him. The rest of us seem to be on the outs for the moment but until we figure out what happened, that's fine. The two of them curl up on the living room rug and I realize it's the first time I've seen them together like that. They are more than Kotah and Keyla, the Prime heirs and sibling survivors. They are pack.

I catch Brant's t-shirt as it gets pitched from above and pull it on. Nothing like starting your day off naked in front of your friends. If only this were an isolated incident. "Does anyone have any idea what the hell is going on?"

Lukas is doing something magical over by the stove and chatting with Hawk. Jaxx is talking in whispered tones with Doc. And our wolf has finally stopped growling.

Brant wraps a strong arm around my shoulder and kisses the side of my head. "So I guess we're the only ones left with nothing to do but watch and worry."

"I'd like another job, please. I don't like this one."

Hawk looks over at us and frowns. "The two of you can pack us up. We leave in ten."

"Wait? What? Where? What's going on?"

Brant looks at me and chuckles. "Wow, that was a lot of questions."

"I have a lot of questions."

Hawk frowns. "We'll shower on the plane. Go-bags and laptops only. Whatever we need so we don't have to come back anytime soon. Brant, get the suspect wall info from the office."

"On it."

Brant heads off and I'm at a loss. I'm so confused. "What does Kotah having an allergy attack and not sleeping have to do with an emergency evac?"

"Kotah has slowly been poisoned," Lukas says. "There are trace elements of shellfish in this cooking spray. There's also something magical lying underneath to bind and compound it. It's too early for me to know more than that."

Hawk is gathering file folders off the kitchen table and shoving them into his computer bag. "Whatever's been happening, his wolf sensed it. Kotah's not safe here. That's why his wolf took over. If we want Kotah back, we need to get him somewhere safe where he can rest and relax."

"Adahy said this might happen. She's been so careful."

Lukas puts the cooking spray into a large ZipLock bag and shrugs. "I doubt we'll get any answers from this, but we'll try. At the very least, I'll focus on the magical signature."

I nod. "Okay dressed and packed to leave in ten. Where are we going?"

Hawk shakes his head. "I'll decide and you'll all find out when we're on the plane. Jaxx, wake your parents. Lukas can take the helicopter and get them home. We're pulling out of the palace completely until we know what the hell we're dealing with."

Jaxx straightens. "Yeah, good luck with that. When Mama finds out someone took a run at one of her boys she'll be locked on us tighter than ever. The only thing wilder than a mama bear is Mama jaguar."

Hawk curses. "Fine. Get them ready for the plane then."

Jaxx nods and pats Doc on the shoulder. "Done deal. Don't leave without us."

Brant

"Some fucking morning, eh?" Doc and I are lounging in two of the four leather captain's chairs near the front of the plane. Keyla and Kotah are curled up on the floor a little further back and Calli and Hawk are with Jaxx and his parents in the aft stateroom relaxing on the two plush couches. "It looked like it was starting okay for you when I interrupted."

Doc raises a dark brow and chuckles. "Interrupted? You mean when you wrecking-balled your way into my suite at the crack of dawn?"

"Hey, I was in an adrenaline rush. I didn't come at it that hard. I blame weak hinges."

Doc chuckles. "Tell that to the kindling that used to be the door to my suite."

I shrug. "No apologies. I'd kill more than a door to save one of my mates."

"I know you would, B."

We both fall quiet as our gazes catch on the two wolves. Where Kotah is a silver timber wolf with rich dark undertones of chocolate brown in his coat, Keyla is such a light silver, she's almost white.

"I can't help thinking they're a lot like us. Siblings brought closer by the cruelties of the world. Two fighters bonding in a struggle to survive."

Doc nods. "The same but different."

"Different how?"

"They didn't have Margo and Ben to keep them whole."

"Amen to that, brother." I hold my fist out and we bump to toast our foster parents.

"Do you honestly think the kid will be okay?"

Doc nods. "Yeah, once his wolf realizes the threat is over, he'll stand down. I've seen this before in wildling war vets. He's just stuck in survival mode and feels less vulnerable in his base form."

"Don't we all."

Hawk and Calli pass by the wolves and come join us. Calli opts to forego a leather seat of her own to curl up in my lap. I snuggle her in and nuzzle her neck.

She wraps her arm around my shoulder and hangs on like she's coming unraveled. A golden swath of hair keeps me from seeing how bad she is. I brush it back and expose her emerald green eyes. She looks tired and sad.

"Anything I can do, beautiful?"

"You're doing it."

"Then I'm happy to keep doing it." I'll hold her for as long as she'll let me and never complain.

"You can do something for me if you don't mind."

I meet Hawk's gaze. "What do you need?"

"When we land, I want you to invite your friend in the FCO

accounting department for dinner tonight. Doc, if you don't mind picking her up at headquarters when she finishes work, I'd rather not draw attention to her meeting with one of us directly."

Doc nods. "So that's where we're headed? Into the belly of the beast?"

"Close to it. I bought a wooded property under one of the shell companies I set up for my mates. I bought it with Kotah in mind and think it'll allow him to run and breathe while I'm in the city. It backs into a forest reserve and is only a twenty-minute helicopter ride from the FCO corporate head office."

I nod. "That's thoughtful. I'm sure it'll help."

Doc looks at me and arches a dark brow. "You have a shell company with properties? Are you holding out on me?"

I shrug. "Hawk mentioned it. I didn't ask."

"Oh, hell. I would've lasted two seconds before curiosity killed me."

Brant shrugged. "That's not why I'm here."

"Sure, buuuut?"

When I say nothing more, Doc frowns at me. "Okay, I'll ask him. What kind of properties? What does Brant own?"

Hawk seems a little hesitant but when he checks with me I shrug. "I have no secrets. And there's no shutting him up now. Go ahead."

Hawk shrugs and sits deeper in the leather seat. "In Brant's trust, there is a residential property on the western seaboard, a chain of youth hostels that focus on getting teens and runaways out of bad situations, a restaurant franchise, a few investments in small businesses I thought he'd appreciate supporting, and a certain, family-owned buffalo ranch that was getting encroached upon by developers and politicians."

I stare at him and blink. "You bought Ben and Margo's ranch?"

"No. *You* ensured Ben and Margo's ranch remains theirs to

own and operate for perpetuity. It has nothing to do with me. It's not my name on the deeds."

"I don't know whether to be grateful or pissed that you did that behind my back."

Hawk shrugs. "If I get a say in the choice, pick grateful."

I chuckle. "You're an ass."

"But?" Calli says, expectantly.

"But you're our ass and yeah, that was thoughtful."

"Restaurants," Doc says. "What kinda menu?"

"Country chicken and ribs."

I nod "Nice. I can get behind that. And I'm looking forward to learning about my youth hostels, too. I have ideas about programs for fae kids having trouble during puberty."

Doc nods. "It's a dangerous time with powers coming into full strength for the first time. How are the kids we rescued doing?"

Hawk sighs. "Of the twelve we rescued, all but three were able to be placed back with their parents. Those are looking good. Two of the three are under supervision to get their powers regulated and one ghosted the moment we got him to the safehouse."

"We lost one?" My bear growls. "You should've told me that, Hawk."

Hawk leans his head back and closes his eyes. "It's hard to keep a kid who can alter air and produce boltholes to other locations. He didn't want to be where we could help him. He knows he's welcome back. There's nothing to tell."

"Was it one of mine? One of the kids I put into the Transitions System?"

"Yes. The male faery who commands energy fields."

"Then you definitely should've told me, Hawk."

He sits up and glares. "And what good does that do? Can you find him? No. Can you fix a kid who doesn't want to be fixed? No. The Black Knight bastards had him for months. There's no telling what kind of mind-altering bullshit they were put through. If there's any chance to intervene, you'll be the first to know. Until then, why should we all worry?"

I sit back and cross my arms. "You still should've told me. It's my fault that kid is mixed up in this."

"No. It's not. That's my point."

"I'd like to be brought up to speed on him."

"I have a dossier with all the information on my laptop. I'll print it for you the first chance I get."

"Speaking of dossiers," Calli says, straightening in my lap. "Hawk, you picked up all the folders on the kitchen table when we left. One of those was the folder of information Mama researched and put together for me about possible fae species who could live on both sides of the portal gate or resurrect on the other side or who knows what."

"In other words, your Riley file," he says, his eyes rolling closed once again. "My bag is in the entrance closet. It'll be in there. You're welcome to get it."

She kisses my nose and does just that. A moment later, she comes back with the information Jaxx's mom dug up for her. As a long-time historian for the fae community, Mama Stanton knows a lot about many of the fae races that didn't settle on this side of the portal gate.

When she comes back, it looks like she's about to take her seat, so I scoop her back into my lap and get her settled the way she was.

"I'm more convinced than ever that Riley is alive and waiting for me on the StoneHaven side of the Portal Gate. That's why I hear her best at the palace. That's close to where the gate is, right?"

"Yeah," I say, skimming the text of what she's going through. "The Bastion, the palace, and the Portal Gate are all in Lebanon Kansas."

"Good. Now, all I have to do is get strong enough so my

phoenix can crack the tab on that sucker and voila, I'm reunited with my bestie."

I pat her thigh. "I hate to be the wet blanket in this fiery phoenix scenario, but we need one more soul crystal before your pendant is complete and your full-power unlocks. Which means... Hawk's up next."

Hawk opens one eye a crack and frowns. "I'm aware."

CHAPTER FOUR

Calli

Hawk's plane touches down outside of Montclair, New Jersey at shortly after three in the afternoon. We divide into three SUVs. Hawk, Mama, and I take the wolves. Lukas is driving Jaxx, his dad, Doc, and Brant in the second truck. And Keyla's two security guys are in the third truck with the two local FCO personal security officers who met us at the airport to watch over Jaxx's parents.

"How long until we get to where we're staying?" I'm not usually a 'are we there yet' kinda passenger, but it's been a long and emotional day.

Hawk reaches over to where I sit in the shotgun seat and squeezes my hand. "Not five minutes. I chose the location specifically for its access to the airfield and because the cul de sac backs into the forest reserve. We'll be there soon."

I look past Maggie sitting in the middle to where the wolves are laying in the back of the truck. "I thought once we got on the plane and Kotah's wolf knew he was safe, he'd relax enough to allow Kotah to come forward again."

Mama reaches forward and takes my hand. "Give him time, sweet girl."

"Time is something we've run out of," Hawk says, following the GPS instructions to turn. "Someone tried to kill him. Was it an attack on the quint or the Prime in Waiting? And speaking of Kotah's destiny, what do we do if the Prime dies before Kotah's in control? If we can't produce the Prime in Waiting for his coronation, we'll be up shit's creek."

I chuckle but there's no humor in it. "When are we *not* up shit's creek? It seems to me we should know how to maneuver those particular rapids by now."

"One would think."

I reach sideways and lace my fingers with Hawk's. "And about what Brant said in the plane about you being up to complete the pendant…"

He pulls his hand free and grips the steering wheel. "I'm aware that things need to be finalized with the quint. I'm doing my best—"

"*Not* what I was saying." I cut off his rant and retake his hand. "I wanted to say that I'm so proud of how far you've come. I don't want you to pressure yourself. Accepting people into your heart and learning to trust someone soul-deep, takes time. I think you're doing great."

He huffs. "The universe has spoken. It's time to open the Portal Gate. To do that, you need to be at full strength. For that to happen you need four, fully-bonded mates."

"And to be fully-bonded, you've got to live and breathe it." I reach up and press my hand to his forehead. "It can't come from here. It has to come from here." I move my hand from his head to his heart.

"That doesn't bode well for the two realms, does it?"

Hawk's right. It doesn't take long to get to where we're going. I'm surprised too. The neighborhood is upscale residential but it's not Hawk's kind of upscale. The cul de sac has seven houses on it, two on each side as you drive in toward the circle, and three houses angled around the circle of the dead end.

Hawk pulls into the open court and slows the truck to a stop. A moment later Lukas pulls up to our left and rolls the passenger window down.

Brant sticks his head out and leans on the window ledge. "Where we headed?"

"Ladies choice," Hawk says, looking back to me. "Which one suits you?"

I look at him and blink. "What? You want me to pick a house? I thought you already bought it."

"I bought *them*. So pick the one you want to stay in."

"You bought *three* houses?"

"Three very *small* houses, yes. I'll tear these down and build something more appropriate. I didn't have time to get everything I wanted to be finished in such a short timeframe."

I roll my eyes, but I should be getting used to this by now. "I like the stone two-story in the middle. Maggie? Which one would you and Jonathan like?"

"We're fine anywhere, son, but the bungalow on the left does remind me of our home in Texas. And it has lovely flowerbeds."

Hawk points out the window. "Jaxx's parents are in that one, Keyla and Doc are in that one, we're in this one." When everyone nods, Hawk drives straight up the driveway and parks in front of the two-car garage. We all bail out and Hawk and I meet at the back bumper.

The moment the hatch opens, Kotah and Keyla hop out. "There are four-hundred acres of protected forest behind the house. Go get some dirt under your claws, Wolf."

The two of them trot off between the houses and I sigh. "I want my sweet prince back."

"I know you do, Spitfire. So do I."

We're still standing there looking sad at one another when we're interrupted by a neighbor.

37

"Hello, newcomers," a soft-middle, silver-haired man says, jogging over. "I'm Andy Mandle. Welcome to Carter Court. Are you folks all together?"

Hawk turns, hand extended. "Hawk Barron, and this is my lovely wife, Calli. It's nice to meet you, Andy. And to answer your question, yes, we're all together."

"Were those wolves? Did I just see you let wolves out of your truck?"

Oh, awesome, nosy neighbors.

Hawk forces a smile. "It must've been the view from your property. Sweet Prince and his younger sister Princess are Alaskan Malamutes. Highly trained and completely domesticated. Nothing to worry about."

"Because we don't allow exotics in Montclair."

"Good to know."

"We also don't allow dogs off-leash."

Hawk rolls his eyes and waves his hand. "Lukas, could you come over here and meet our neighbor, please."

Lukas strides over from where he's speaking with the four security officers. "Yes, sir?"

Hawk straightens. "This is Andy Mandle our new neighbor. He's awfully concerned that we know all the rules of this road. Could you please reassure him there's nothing to worry about and escort him back to his property, please."

"Of course. I'll take care of it."

Lukas escorts Andy back the way he came and I don't even care enough to ask what he'll do with him.

I'm too tired to care.

Once inside, my bag plops onto the floor of the master bedroom and I check out the space. The house is freshly furnished with the linens stacked on the bed still in the plastic.

There's nothing of us here.

It's stupid. I should be used to drifting from place to place. I lived most of my life from a backpack until Riley and I got our shithole apartment. Why aren't I happy to be here?

I remember Kotah showing us into our Timber Trails Suite at the palace and loving it instantly. It spoke to me. It was Kotah and it exuded his love.

My feet wander the room, my mind only partially engaged in where I am.

The oversized windows face out on the sea of bushy green behind the house and my heart sinks. I drop to my knees at the low window ledge and rest my chin on my folded arms.

The trees sway with the pull of a gentle breeze and I search for a glimpse of Kotah and Keyla's beautiful, thick, coats. Nothing. Wherever my wolf is, he's not here.

I'm losing him.

My chest tightens as the familiar ache of the past two months overwhelms. I'm as useless to him as I was the day I found Riley. There's nothing I can do. It's one of those slow-motion moments when you know your heart is breaking but there's nothing to be done to fix it.

I brush away hot tears and draw a shuttered breath.

"Hey now, kitten. Enough of that." Jaxx lifts me off the floor and hugs me tight. "What's this about?"

I force a laugh. "Ignore me. I'm being emotional."

Brant and Hawk are both there too, looking worried.

"Seriously, just a momentary lapse. I'm good. Let's get this place set up. Lots to do. Busy. Busy."

I move to leave but Jaxx won't have it. The pure love in his beautiful turquoise gaze nearly does me in. I hold up my finger and blink fast. "Don't look at me like that, puss."

"Like what? Like I love you? Like I'd slay any monster that dared to make the female of my soul cry? I would... and I will. Say the word and it'll be done."

"Tell us, Spitfire," Hawk says, easing closer. "We not only sense your pain, we feel it. What brought on the tears?"

JL MADORE

I turn back to look out the window and sigh. "When I found Riley in that alley, the life we were building shattered. All the hope and excitement of getting off the street, of the two of us building something… it fell apart in front of my eyes. There was nothing I could do."

"You got even," Brant says. "We got Sonny and his gang and shut down the guns and trafficking of women along that stretch. The Sons are done."

"I think she means nothing to do to save the dream of a new life," Jaxx says, pressing his lips against my forehead.

"Nothing's falling apart here," Hawk says.

I shrug. "Just now, I stared into the woods and tried to send Kotah my love. I can't feel him. He's the first one I connected with. He's always been so easy for me to feel, his emotions so steady and reassuring. Now… he's lost."

"He won't be for long. Trust me, Spitfire. Kotah's a lot tougher than he looks. He'll fight his way back to us. I've talked to him more than once about the quint. There's nothing in the two realms he wants more than our family."

"Me too," I choke out. "Gawd, I love you guys so much. But the universe makes it a habit of taking things away from me. What if this is another cruel, cosmic joke and the shoe is about to drop?"

"Not gonna happen." Brant tugs me free of Jaxx's arms and hugs me until I can't breathe. "You picked us and now you're stuck with your choices."

With Brant's height and bulk, I'm practically swallowed up by my bear. That's fine. I don't mind at all.

Hawk takes hold of me next. He chucks my chin and his still gray eyes peg me in place. I used to think they were cold and held no feeling. I couldn't have been more wrong.

Hawk's eyes hold nothing *but* emotion. And now that we are past the walls of hostility he defended himself with, there's nothing but miles of hope, compassion, and fear.

I'd never call him on the fear because I know he fears the same thing I do... that this will be taken away from us.

"He could've *died* today," I whisper. The words burn like acid on my tongue.

The dip in Hawk's chin is almost imperceptible. "But he didn't. We'll figure out who did it."

"And get even." I make sure my murderous expectations are plain in my expression. "People will learn they don't take what's mine. If they try—they die."

All three of them nod. This time around, neither Brant nor Jaxx balk at the idea that I mean it. My resolve to keep them safe is no less committed than theirs to me.

After another deep breath, I swipe my cheeks with both palms and dry my hands on my pants. "Okay, first things first. Where's the office? I want to set up our suspect wall and get back on track.

Hawk nods. "Main floor. I'll show you where."

Jaxx

After Hawk takes Calli down to the office to get set up, Brant and I undo the bags of sheets, towels, and whatnots. "There's a grocery delivery down in the kitchen. I saw laundry soap and fabric softener. Can you grab it? I don't want Calli sleeping on scratchy, fresh from the store sheets."

"On it."

I noticed an upstairs washer and dryer at the end of the hall and take the linens in there to get started.

"Hey, baby boy," Mama says, coming up to join me. She's got the jugs of laundry soap and softener I sent Brant for and I have no doubt she commandeered them without giving him the option to turn her down. "Let me do that."

"I've got it, Mama."

She nods. "I have no doubt you do. Busy work has always been your way when there's trouble in the air. Now, go join your mates in the office and figure out who did this to my sweet boy."

Mama faces off with the washer like the force she is and I kiss her cheek. "I learned busy work from you, Mama."

Her smile is stiff. "Yes, you did. Now figure out who's behind this, Jaxxy. No more close calls."

I see the violence stirring in Mama's gaze and hear it in her voice. I know enough not to argue. Mama is the all-time sweetest and warmest woman on the planet but if you fuck with her cubs you lose more than a limb. "Love you, Mama."

"Love you more, baby boy."

∽

Hawk

By six o'clock the houses are settling, and Brant, Doc, and I take the helicopter into Manhattan to meet with Brant's contact in accounting. By six-thirty Brant and I are alone in a private room of an Italian restaurant a few blocks from the FCO head-quarters awaiting their arrival.

"I take it by the way the maître d' greeted you that you own this place?" Brant finishes spreading his napkin over his lap and gestures to the room.

"No. I just like it here. Great food. Great service."

"Mmm, that's nice to hear."

I stand as Carina Scapetti steps into the room. Brant rises as well, and I don't blame him for his mouth falling open.

Carina is a breath-stealing, long-legged, brunette, and the scarlet, crushed velvet dress clinging to her curves could stop a man's heart. "Sit, baby," she says, eyeing Brant up and down. "I'm Carina."

When she offers her hand, Brant doesn't miss a beat. He gathers her fingers in his snow-shovel hands and plants his lips. "A pleasure to meet you, beautiful. Now I see why Hawk said this is one of his favorite places."

"Mmm, another playboy. Two of you in one of my private rooms. Lucky me." She winks and sidles her way over to touch my shoulder. "So, after you drop off the map for what now, almost six weeks, you bring me an apology?"

I chuckle knowing exactly where Carina thinks this is going. "Apologies, *bella*. Brant and I are both off the market. I'm afraid our private room wining and dining days are over."

She pushes out her red, painted lips in an adorable pout and I realize how deeply Calli's hold on me goes.

I'm not even tempted.

I remember all the highlights of those lips and how good it could be with Carina and nothing within me is interested. I admit I'm surprised. I worried I might screw up or self-sabotage if things got tough.

It's a relief to know I'm all-in with my phoenix.

"Over sounds final, Barron. How over are we talking?"

Brant chuckles. His brow is arched as if he's reading me and finds my mental meandering amusing. Can he sense my revelations? He surely smells that my attraction hasn't risen. "Yeah, Barron, how over are we talking? Just how off the market are we?"

I arch a brow and flash him a droll smile. I can read him too and I know where he's going. "Really?"

"Oh, yeah, I think so." He waggles his brows. "You're up, remember? Time to put up or shut up."

Carina shifts her weight on her Stillettos. "What am I missing?"

Brant says nothing—he doesn't have to—the challenge clear

in his gaze. Fine. If it makes him happy. I toss my napkin onto the table and stand. He does the same.

Brant and I haven't had any one-on-one but as he says—it's time to put up or shut up.

Carina is human. She can't smell Brant's mating scent flaring, but I can. *Fuck.*

It's a blend of his mated scents.

He's got the sweet, feminine succulence of Calli, the wild spice of Jaxx, and the earthy warmth of Kotah respiring from his skin. My hawk recognizes those scents as home. And yeah, now that I'm committed to this little PDA, it's a lot easier than I thought to ramp up.

Rarely have I ever had a tryst with any female as tall as I am. I can count those moments on one hand. But Brant and I look straight into one another's gaze. I study the emotions swirling in those golden eyes of his. On the outside, everything with Brant is a game. When I look closer, I see the truth.

He wants more.

"You sure about this, Bear?"

"Don't I look sure?"

He does. I guess it's me who's not. There's something exotically sexy about having our first kiss in public and in front of one of my ex-lovers.

I slide my fingers under his brunette waves and grip his neck, pulling him closer until we're chest to chest. His pecs are broad and it's like cozying up against a brick wall.

"Oh, like that, is it?" Carina says.

"It is," I say, not breaking focus on where I'm headed.

I tilt my head and seal our fate. Brant's lips are hot and welcoming. I don't know what I expect from him, but the sheer hunger and submission of him letting me nail him against the wall and practically shove my tongue down his throat isn't it.

He submits but he's not completely submissive. Holding his

own, his tongue thrusts and parries fighting for dominance. He's a good kisser, I'll give him that.

Brant's hand is hard on my lower back. Rough fingers splay against my spine and pull my hips forward to meet the solid steel of his cock.

My hawk shrieks shrill in my head.

The uptick of my pulse is directly related to that cock and suddenly I don't give two shits about dinner or the girl from accounting or the fact that we're not alone. Honestly, the 'not alone' part adds fuel to the fire.

He's willing and I could unbuckle his belt, drop his slacks, and fuck him over the focaccia basket right now.

He slips his hand between us and palms the front of my pants. *Fuck.* I'm hard and hungry for more. I did not see this coming. There are still times I barely like the guy.

Before clothes start shredding and things get out of hand, I ease back. "Raincheck."

"Done. When and where?"

I draw a deep breath and I like the scent of him on my skin. Yeah. It's been an emotional day.

Carina doesn't seem the least bit satisfied with the end of the show.

If I'm being honest—neither am I.

"Well, well." She swallows, waving a menu in front of her face. "That changes nothing for me, Barron. In my restaurant, the customer is always right."

Brant chuckles. "It would've been spectacular, beautiful. Unfortunately—or actually no—very fortunately we have a full bed. Thank you, though. Your offer is appreciated."

"Well, you two know where I am if you change your minds." Carina takes her leave to check on her other customers and the two of us reclaim our seats.

Brant sinks into his chair, a sexy smirk warming his expression. "As far as firsts go, that was memorable."

"I'll give you that." What I don't mention is that I'm still thinking about his cock. I know he's a big boy. We're all naked enough that even though I've never taken advantage of Brant's offerings, I'm well aware.

I know he's been a player, too. I have no doubt he can fuck. He doesn't have the wild and powerful edge Jaxx does, but I bet he'd be a damn good lay.

Brant texts someone and hits me with a hot look. "If they're more than fifteen minutes out, we're locking that door and rainchecking it like you fucking read about."

"I'm on board with that."

The reply text comes back and I'm stroking the front of my slacks like a horny Pavlov's dog. "How long."

"They're here."

"Fuck me."

"Yeah… well no. Whatever. I'm disappointed."

Me too. I straighten my napkin over my lap, draw a deep breath, and groan. "Tell me she's not a wildling. This room smells like we bathed in sexual tension."

"Brownie."

"From what sect?"

"Irish."

I let out a sigh of relief. The *brunaidh* are known for extraordinary hard work, low-level magic, and wild tempers if taken for granted, but they don't have heightened senses. She won't be able to smell the sex in the air.

"Doc will," Brant says, following my train of thought.

I shrug. "Yeah, well, I suspect over the years he's seen, smelled, and participated in enough sexual encounters with you that he won't have a problem with it.

Brant chuckles. "You might be right there. It would take a lot to shock him."

For the first time, I'm curious to hear what kind of sex-capades Brant got up to in his wilder days.

When the pocket door slides open, Doc escorts in a petite girl with wide brown eyes and wavy pink hair.

"KadeeLi, it's good to see you," Brant says, standing to hug her. It doesn't slip my notice that he side-hugs her and retreats to sit down immediately replacing his napkin and tucking back under the table.

I take his cue and do the same. After shaking her hand, I seat her across from me and get things tucked away ASAP.

Doc looks from Brant to me and back to his bear brother. "And now I understand the text about us possibly running late." He laughs and takes his seat across from Brant. "So, what did we miss?"

Asshole.

CHAPTER FIVE

Calli

$\mathcal{M}$ama and I get dinner pulled together and I have to admit even though it's a somber affair, Jaxx is right, his mom's southern fried chicken and biscuits can cure what ails you. I eat too much and feel bloated and gross by the time we get through the peach cobbler she baked for dessert. Until Jaxx, a full dinner followed by dessert was unheard of in my life.

"Being mated to you is going to make me fat, Jaxx." I plunk into the office chair after the Stanton's clear out. I pat my belly and regret my lack of impulse control.

Then I pick up my abandoned bag of M&Ms.

Jaxx laughs. "Wildlings don't get fat, kitten. Our bodies run the metabolism of two symbiotic creatures. That takes a lot of juice. We burn up calories like you eat M&Ms—with keen efficiency."

I toss one across the desk at him.

He dives a couple of inches to the side and makes the save from my bad throw.

"Oh, you only said that so I'd throw one at you."

His smile is wicked sexy. "You're catching on."

"And then there's the sex."

Jaxx blinks. "What's that now?"

"For burning calories. Our dual metabolisms as well as all the sex."

He nods. "Yeah. There's that."

I set the bag of M&M's down before I barf and rock back in my chair. "Speaking about sex with you."

He laughs. "My favorite subject. Go on."

I giggle as he bites his bottom lip. So playful my puss. "How's Hawk doing? I'm not asking for details... just broad strokes. You guys had another solo play session and it felt like things were twanging in a good way last night. Are we gaining ground with him?"

Jaxx's smile is too freaking adorable. When he rubs his chest as if his heart aches, I melt. "You're falling hard for him, aren't you?"

"Past tense. It's too late for me. I love him hard. And to answer your question, yeah... he's doing great."

I let out a heavy sigh. "Good. I'm glad to hear that."

"Then why don't you look or sound glad? You're okay with Hawk and I, right? We talked about it, but if something changed you gotta let me know."

I wave that away. "Aside from a little frustration about being left out of your fun, it's only that I'm scared."

"Still worried about the universe taking us away?"

I blink at the sting behind my eyes. "I've never been a needy woman, but with you guys and my history..."

The click of claws against hardwood brings Kotah into the office. He plods straight over to me and sets his head in my lap. "Hey, sweet prince. How are you feeling?"

I run my fingers through the long, guard hairs of his coat

and deep into the velvety fur underneath. I start slow and make sure the snappy, growly wolf is done with his mood.

He lets off a sad whine and my tears push harder.

I stop fighting them. If there's something that my healing tears can do for Kotah, I'll cry for both of us.

Bending at the waist I snuggle my wolf and set my worry from earlier free. "When I saw you on the floor and Hawk trying to revive you... my heart shattered. I love you, Kotah. More than even I realized. I love you and need you to come back to us."

I let my tears dampen the top of his head and his ears. His soft whine breaks my heart. He's not shifting back and I don't know if that's because he can't or he won't.

Either way, it hurts. "Whatever time you need, sugar, when you come back to us we'll be here waiting."

"Damn straight." Jaxx is there, right beside us on his knees. "Can I get in on this love-in, Wolf? You shook me up pretty badly this morning. I could use a hug too."

Kotah's wolf makes no move to accept him but doesn't growl either. I shrug. "I think that's a yes."

"I'll take it." Jaxx slides forward and curls himself around our mate. "I love you, Kotah. I know you're in there somewhere and you can hear me. I love you. Hang in there. We'll figure this out."

Hawk

After an illuminating dinner with KadeeLi, I dismiss Doc for the night. I ask him to drive her home and then he's free to drive back to Montclair to be with Keyla. Brant and I walk the few city blocks to the FCO head office to follow up on a few things we learned.

"Okay, give me the key players," Brant says as we navigate the flow of early evening foot traffic.

"Jayne Trenton. She's a Manhattan socialite and business shark. You met at the Bastion."

"Not really. I heard the stories, though."

"Right. You were compelled by Calli. Okay, Jayne has been my Personal Assistant for years and is shrewd in business. She's tough and cold and—"

"—the female version of you?"

I consider that and nod. "Pretty much."

"Do you think she's capable of fucking with your accounts the way KadeeLi described?"

"Capable, yes. Do I think she would do it? No. Jayne's all about running FCO to the moon. We worked well together because she's passionate about the company. She's driven enough to be underhanded but it would hurt the company. I can't see her doing that."

"Okay then, who?"

"That's the million-dollar question."

"Give me another player."

"That's just it. I vet my people. If I didn't know this was happening, there's no way I would've believed that anyone within my inner circle of management would do this."

"Humor me."

"Okay... Hunter Gable, my Director of Operations. Coyote shifter, Yale grad, good instincts."

"And you two get along?"

"I thought we did. This whole situation has me second-guessing all my relationships."

"Okay, next?"

"Tanis Marx is in charge of legal and compliance."

"Marx? As in the Guild of Mages Marx family?"

"The same. Tanis has always been a bit of a pain in my ass, but a solid company man."

"Pain in your ass how?"

"We view the directives of the company differently. I've always wanted FCO to be a company of the people for the people. He's more capitalistic in his thinking. Lesser Fae are less powerful and therefore less important. That sort of thing."

"That's bullshit."

"From a moral standpoint, it is. From a business perspective, I understand his arguments to cater to the members of the community who hold more power. I just don't agree."

"But it's your company."

"Yep."

"Who else?"

"Chadwick Sands should be mentioned, I suppose."

"And who's he?"

"He handles international affairs. We rarely see eye-to-eye and there have been times we've butted heads. He has pushed me for years to go public and take on a board of directors."

"But again, it's your company."

"Yep." I make my way around a couple with a stroller and come back to the convo. "Why would I go public? I certainly don't need more money and I won't let someone derail what I've built."

We stop at the lights opposite my building and I take it in. For the past decade, there's nothing I loved more than to stand in this spot and see all that concrete and glass stretching up to the blue sky.

At this moment, I'm still proud and possessive... but the passion doesn't touch the fueled focus I have for my mates and our calling to unite the realms.

"Are we walking here or waiting for the next one?"

I meet Brant's gaze and he's gesturing to the crosswalk emptying of people.

"Sorry, yep. Hustle, it's not a long light."

The two of us jog across and are hopping onto the curb as the cars rev up and roll behind our heels.

Brant stops when we're right in front of the building and smiles. "You know, it's been a goal of mine for years to come here on a mission of importance."

"A mission of importance?"

"Yeah, you know. I could've come for the yearly open house or to pick up a new vehicle for my district office, but I wanted my first time here to be me as a man with a purpose."

I chuckle and step under the iron and glass entrance. "I guess you got your wish. Uniting the two realms, sussing out who's manipulating the Fae Prime and Council, and doing that while saving one mate from ruination and another from a plot of assassination."

Brant pushes through the glass turnstile and chuckles. "I guess I did. Careful what you wish for, right?"

"Sir Barron, welcome back, sir."

I head over to the security desk and shake hands with the night guard. "How are things with the night crew, Mallory?"

"Always a pleasure, sir,"

I nod and introduce him to Brant. "Mallory Daniford this is Brant Robbins, one of my mates. I assume the news of me marked as a Guardian to the Phoenix has spread. You're aware that's why I've been absent?"

"Oh, yes sir. Lady Jayne sent a company memo explaining everything. We're all so proud to know you're one of the chosen. The two realms couldn't hope for a finer male at the helm."

I squeeze his shoulder and he smiles. As a member of the hulderfolk, not many people make contact with them. He's always appreciated that I'm neither afraid to touch him or hiding anything when I do.

The hulderfolk are a walking lie detector race. They can't lie and they sense lies in others. Perfect for security.

"Mallory, tell me. Over the course of time while I've been gone, has anything struck you as odd or out of rhythm with the norm?"

"Odd, sir?"

"Yes. New faces coming and going. Odd deliveries. People changing the routine of hours. That sort of thing."

He seems to consider that for a bit and then shakes his head. "The strangest thing was not seeing you here day and night, sir."

"And Lady Jayne," Brant says. "She's working the same as always?"

Mallory looks at me and I nod. "It's okay. Brant and I are working on the same problem."

"Problem, sir?"

"Can the three of us speak privately, Mallory?"

"Of course, sir." He steps around the desk and stands next to Brant and I. A moment later, his tail extends and uncoils, encircling us until he's wrapped the three of us within a circle of three feet. "You can speak privately now, sir."

"And you'll keep everything between us."

"Of course, sir."

Good. I didn't think Mallory would be involved. I tell Mallory about the misappropriation of funds and the kidnapping of the teens and how everything is being made to look like me. Then I mention the Black Knight and how our quint has been attacked and sabotaged a half-dozen times over the past weeks. "Someone doesn't want Calli to open the portal gate and they're willing to kill to stop it."

"I appreciate sharing your confidence, sir, but why tell me? I just work the door."

I chuckle. "A machine is only as strong as its cogs, Mallory. I value you and all my support staff as greatly as my executives... oftentimes more."

He beams at the praise. "How can I be of help, sir?"

"I'm taking control of things again and I'm betting that when

I do, someone will be angry enough to start showing their true colors. Let me know if you see any new faces or if someone comes in at an odd hour or anything piques your curiosity." I reach over his desk and write my private cell number on the pad. "This number is only for my mates and most trusted friends. I'll always answer it. If you have anything to tell me, call night or day."

"Will do."

"Thank you. And send my love to Marta and the brood."

When Mallory coils his tail behind his back and resumes his place at the night desk, Brant and I head to the elevators. I catch Brant eyeing me up and shrug. "What?"

"You genuinely like that guy."

"Mallory? Of course, I do. He's been with me for eight years. And every night for those eight years I worked late. We've had many midnight conversations."

"He's a blue-collar worker."

"So?"

Brant chuckles. "So, nothing. You just surprised me."

The elevator dings and the doors slide open. We step in and I slide my keycard into the slot as I push the button for the upper floors. "I suppose me surprising you is a good thing?"

"It is." When the doors close, he leans back and flashes me a heated grin. "So, your office. You got a couch in there?"

I blink. My mind is deep in the spin of reclaiming my company and I miss the segue into my office furniture. "My office? What?"

"A couch. I—"

The elevator doors open on twelve and Penelope from Property Rights steps on. Her arms are full and overflowing with folders and she startles when she looks up and sees me. "Mr. Barron... you have a guest. I'm so sorry. I should've taken another car."

She sends an apologetic look to Brant but he waves that away. "You're good. Here. It looks like…"

Brant reaches to steady the stack of files just as she loses control of them. Thank the Powers for large hands and quick reflexes. He gets her straightened up in no time.

"What keeps you here so late, Penny?" I ask

"I'm working copying the deed information for the land and property transfers."

"What land and property transfers?"

Her eyes widen. "The seizures of the fae reservation lands finalizing next week."

Now I'm the one bugging out. "Excuse me. FCO is initiating land seizures? On what grounds?"

"Failure to thrive?"

"How many of them?"

"All fifty-two states."

I press my palm over my mouth to keep from saying something hugely inappropriate and highly offensive in front of one of my female, junior staff.

Thankfully, Brant intercedes before the top of my head splatters the inside of the elevator. "How and when were you put on this task?"

Penny looks stricken. "I thought…" The door opens on eighteen and she's got the look of a deer caught in the headlights. She looks to the three people working in legal and then back to us. "We got emails weeks ago. After hours only, not to affect our daily work…"

I gesture for her to exit and Brant and I follow her onto the eighteenth floor. "How many of you are working on the seizure of the fae reservation lands?"

All three of them raise their hands.

"And who authorized it?"

"You did, sir."

Brant

Hawk storms off down the hall and a moment later the air is filled with the crashing of heavy objects, the smashing of glass, and some of the best runs of unfiltered profanity I've ever had the pleasure to hear uttered. Seriously, it would make a marine blush.

The four employees look terrified.

"So, hey, it's nice to meet you. I'm Brant, one of your bosses quint mates. As you probably gathered, he never ordered the seizure of the land and is a bit overwhelmed at the moment."

"We got emails…" a meek, blond guy says. "Do you think we're fired?"

"Nah, definitely not fired," I say, with a fair amount of certainty. "Hawk's been identity hacked within the company, and someone is moving his cheese. It's why we're here. Something of the corporate espionage nature is underfoot. The land seizure is likely only one act of destruction. Have any of you or your colleagues worked on anything else over the past two months that seems counter to what Hawk would want?"

They still look panicked. "Is that a yes?"

Cue the chirp of crickets.

"Okay, speak up. Can we start a dialogue here, please?"

Hawk comes back from down the hall and he looks like he was gobbled up in a hurricane and shit out the tail end. I brush a crazy Einstein patch of hair down and he draws a deep breath. "Better?"

He nods. "Me—minutely better. The conference room—not so much. Remind me to call maintenance."

I chuckle and turn to the peanut gallery. "Okay, everyone, from the top. Let's chat. What the fuck is going on?"

~

Jaxx

One of the boons of the house Calli picked for us to stay in is the sunken Jacuzzi in the back deck. It's tucked behind a wooden screen hanging thick with grapevine and very private. The two of us are nakey and enjoying the jets while Kotah lays quietly on the deck beside us.

The best part is that when Calli's phone goes off, she stands up and bends over the back of the hot tub, her belly on a towel and her ass and hoohaw glistening wet in the moonlight for my pleasured viewing.

"Okay, broody. Try not to kill anyone... I'll tell them."

Calli hangs up from her call with Hawk and frowns. "They've stepped into a shitstorm at the office and aren't coming home tonight. Hawk said there's no danger, just a long night of research and digging through the shit heaping upon his company and his name."

"Does he want us to come into the city and help?"

"He said no, but I'm thinking if they aren't here in the morning, we get dressed to impress and join the fun."

"Done deal."

"What do you think, Kotah?" Calli turns back to the deck and reaches to scratch his ears.

Gawd... all her glistening girl parts. The view is too much for me not to pounce. "Don't move, kitten. Stay right there and let me take advantage of the view."

I'm across the water with my mouth on her core in two beats of a throbbing cock. I nudge her a little higher out of the tub and lick my way through the folds of her pussy. The water has altered the taste of her with chemicals and my jaguar doesn't like it.

Calli has a very distinct taste and smell to her skin. It's become another part of the many reasons I love her.

I let my jaguar prowl forward, a purr rattling out of my chest. The sound triggers a creamy release against my tongue and I lap it up. "I could eat you out all night long and never get enough."

"Mmm, that's how I feel about cock-sucking." She lifts her fanny a little and grinds against my face.

"I guess that's why they invented the sixty-nine."

"Someone should give that woman a medal."

I chuckle. "You think a woman came up with it?"

"Hells yeah."

I'm not getting enough from below, so I roll her onto her back and spread her thighs. With a tight grip at the back of both her knees, I spread her wide and take my time.

Calli's eyes roll closed and she gets busy enjoying the build of her orgasm. She doesn't notice that our wolf is sitting up on his elbows watching.

That's it, Kotah. You're in there. Come join us, buddy.

I meet his gaze and smile at him, then shift my focus back to tonguing our mate. My two fingers inside her start a slow and easy pump and retreat. Her clit is sensitive tonight and I have to back things up a bit so I don't make her crazy.

"Kotah and Brant must've worked you good last night."

"Mhmm... so good."

My jaguar purrs louder. It's a complicated thing balancing multiple mates. As much as I hate that I missed out on Calli, Kotah, and Brant having fun last night, dominating Hawk blows my mind.

The total power he gives me is such a rush.

After a little gentle coaxing, Calli's hips relax and we're good to go harder. I press my tongue on the tight bundle of nerves and flick and swirl, nuzzle and suck.

Man, I love my job.

The scent of the hot tub water is gone and now I'm surrounded by the scent of her feminine cream, the char of her wildling side, and the mating scents of the four of us.

Sometimes I swear my heart will burst.

Hydrogen.

Calli groans, her breath catching as her pelvis rolls. "That feels so good, Jaxx."

I purr against her clit. It isn't so much planned to get her off as a fun side effect. The oscillation of my breath vibrating my tongue as it escapes works in much the same way as a sex toy, giving her an added pleasure.

Her knees tighten and I refuse to let them close. I press her open wider, stretching her, exposing her everything to the night sky above.

"All right, now. Let go and let loose, kitten." I push my tongue against her clit again and purr long and low.

The convulsions of her orgasm light off almost immediately. Her back arches, her damp tits glistening in the moonlight, and her breath catches deep in her throat.

"Yes... oh, yes."

Her inner muscles grab hold of my fingers and pulse with a greedy squeeze. So perfect.

Her first orgasm of the night rolls through her and it's such a relief. After the emotion of the day to be able to shatter her into waves of steamy, creamy ecstasy is a welcome end.

Her head drops back to the towel and I gauge the pulsing constrictions squeezing my fingers. When the ebbing tightening of her orgasm slows, I get out of the tub, scoop her into my arms, and carry her inside.

"I was enjoying the night air," she says, pushing her lip out into a pout.

I chuckle and wait until Kotah is inside before closing the door behind us. "And would you still enjoy it if you knew my parents came outside their house next door to take a midnight skinny dip in the pool in their back yard?"

"*No.* They didn't hear me, did they?"

I laugh and look around the new layout. "No, but I don't want to hear them either. Besides, I'm about to fuck you hoarse, so I thought you'd prefer to be out of earshot."

"Yes, thank you."

With no destination in mind, I lean in and kiss her hard. She meets me just as hungrily, groaning into my mouth and digging her fingers into the muscle of my shoulders.

Damn, she gets me horny.

Setting her on her feet, I smack her ass.

"Ouch, puss. What was that for?"

"That's your cue to run, kitten. New game. It's called Run, Hunt, Fuck." My creativity spirals and all sorts of imaginative inspiration comes to mind. "You run. Kotah and I chase you down. We fuck you and then you run again." I smack her ass again and smile at the pink flesh. "You've got to the count of five. One. Two…"

Calli squeals and takes off running.

"Three. Four. Five. Ready or not, here we come." I pat Kotah's shoulder and let him take the lead. Our senses are keener in our animal forms and Kotah's wolf has the strongest sense of smell out of all of us. Maybe engaging him in a playful mate sex game will bring him out of his current state.

"That's it, Wolf. Breathe her in and track her down so we can claim our prize."

The spring in Kotah's step tells me I'm on to something. He's coming back around. Things are looking up.

CHAPTER SIX

Hawk

"What do you think of that one?"

Brant checks his phone and nods. "Yeah, I think that'll do it. Let me send it to your email and you can upload it."

I move from sitting by the lamp in my meeting area over to my desk and pull up a browser. After verifying the video we shot, I upload it to the CFO server and set it for midnight distribution. Checking my watch, I nod. "Okay, with legal aware of what's going on and halting all things unauthorized, and this going out in just over two hours, I'd say we've taken great strides in ruining someone's night."

Brant chuckles and brings us over two pink drinks that look like something a sorority girl would order.

I arch a brow. "I stock a full bar, you know? Single malt, Irish whiskey, bourbon, cognac, red and white wine."

"Oh, I know. I made these special."

"Uh-huh." I accept mine and take a tentative sip. It's something Calli will enjoy. It's fruity and has a kick. "I'm afraid to ask what this is called. Does it have one of those seductive names like the Damp Panty or the Buttery Nipple?"

"Now that you mention it, it does. I call it the Corporate Blowjob." I cough on my next sip and Brant chuckles. "You did offer me a raincheck. I'm willing to bet, after two or three of these, you and I will be fucking like animals."

I swig back the glass and he matches me. "I'm in the middle of a life crisis. Is now the time to liquor me up for a blowjob? We've got hours of emails to track and files to look through. I'm not leaving this office until that video goes out."

He grabs the stainless steel pitcher from the bar and pours us each a freshie. "Exactly. I'm merely suggesting that a break in the tension will allow us to focus with fresh eyes and an altered perspective."

I accept the second glass of Corporate Blowjob and Brant hits the door and locks us in. "I happen to give a great blowjob and from Kotah's collapse to corporate raiders, I figure you could use the release."

I suck back the second glass and feel the burn of liquid sedation taking hold already. "Wow, how much booze did you put in these?"

"A lot." He chuckles and stands before me, offering his hand. "Raincheck."

I swallow, my mind heavy with a dozen other things. "I'm not saying no, Bear, but maybe now isn't the best time. I'm edgy and—"

Brant reaches for the top button of his dress shirt and sets it free from its mooring. When that's done he moves down and repeats. "I'm getting naked. You don't mind, do you?"

I chuckle, pick up the pitcher and refill my glass. "Why do I have the feeling it doesn't matter what my answer is. In the end, we're ending up naked and fucking."

"Now you're catching on." His shirt falls open and then he

unlatches his belt. "I'm assuming you've got supplies in here somewhere?"

I sip at the edge of the glass and point to the wall cabinet. "Last door on the left. It's got a keypad lock inside. The code is 5492."

"You lock your lube in a safe?" His pants are off and he tosses them over the back of one of the leather side chairs. Brant goes commando under everyday clothes but not under his dress clothes. I share his logic.

"I lock my personal things away from public view and opinion. You may find more than a bottle of lube in there."

Brant arches a brow and saunters over. "May I?"

I raise my glass, taking in the view. He's one helluva lot of man, that's for sure. And for me, a guy who only a week ago opened the door to male/male possibilities, I have to remind myself how much being with Jaxx has broadened my view on pleasure.

"Oh, toys too."

I chuckle at the delight in his voice. "Have you wondered what Jaxx and I did last night in the Den of Debauchery?"

"Wondered? More like obsessed." He straightens with a couple of bottles, a couple of toys, and a box of condoms. "You are hella prepared here."

I finish round three and walk the empty glasses over to the bar to set them out of the way. "Before all of this started I worked hard and played harder."

Brant takes a look around the space. "Any preferences? Position? View?"

I unbuckle my belt and point to the panel beside the bar. "This way, Bear. If you think my supply cupboard is exciting, you're going to blow your load in here." At the end of the bar, I move the teak case I had built to house the first bottle of Dom Perignon I bought. It was supposed to be my reward for reaching the top of my career but every time I achieve what I think my goal is, I make a new goal. It's a good thing champagne ages well. I might never be satisfied.

I place my hand on the scanner hidden behind the case and the panel to my private chamber glides open.

"Welcome, Hawk Barron," the automated system says.

I grab Brant's clothes from the back of the chair and move the party into the private section. "Obsessed you say. Well, if you're interested—"

"Fuck *yes*. Interested doesn't begin to cover it." His gaze jumps around the room, and his hand grips his stiff cock. I don't miss the rough tug as he takes it all in. "I can't believe you have a private fuck pad right in your office."

"No?"

"Well, I can… but holy hell."

"Like I said. I work hard and play harder."

The lights are still off, the chrome and mirrors of the space picking up the lights of the city below. With both of us wildlings, there's no need for lights, but I go around the room and light a few black wax candles for ambiance. "This is a standard sex dungeon if you're wondering. Nothing too hardcore. Just basic BDSM kink."

Brant chuckles. "And what does hardcore look like?"

"It's darker. I've dabbled at clubs a few times but prefer this. It gets addictive, so you have to be sure about what you want from the onset."

He swallows and smiles. "Give me the tour."

I work on the buttons of my shirt as we tour the room. "There's a small washroom through the mirrored door behind me. The bondage couch you might recognize—I ordered the same one for the suite—those are suspension bars, milking table, wall cross, fuck platform, swing, toys, masks, candles, floggers, whips, etcetera."

"What's that?"

"A queening chair. Since we don't have a female here, we don't need that."

He tilts his head, trying to figure it out.

I chuckle. "The female sits in it like a throne and the male lays beneath her, face up."

"*Ohhhh*, it's a sit on my face stool."

"In essence, yes." I let him take it all in. Considering that he's the one who razzed me at the beginning about me not being aware of the possibilities, I'm surprised this seems so foreign and exciting to him. "Have you played with kink before, Bear?"

"Fuzzy handcuffs and vibrators, yeah. Nothing like this though. Fuck, my balls are tingling with cum and we're only on the tour."

After hanging his clothes on a hook by the door, I close us in. I slide my shirt off and hang it on the suit butler beside the door. My pants and socks are next. With the two of us naked, this is suddenly becoming very real.

Why am I nervous? I was ready to ravish him a few hours ago without a second thought. I've never been nervous in this room before. This is my domain.

"This cityscape is incredible."

"It is." I built the room with the cityscape on one wall and mirrored the other three walls and ceiling. The effect is stunning. It's like the lights of the city are coming at you from all sides. "So, this is me."

"Yeah. And I'm impressed."

Okay, good. I breathe a little easier and then I get it. The reason I'm nervous. I care what he thinks. As alien as that is for me, I want this to go well. I want him to accept me and kink is a big part of me.

I point to the table at the end of the bed. "You can put your supplies down."

He does and runway turns for one final spin. Pointing at the large monitor mounted in the corner, he frowns. "What's that? You don't tape people do you?"

I wave away his censure. "No. Never. There are enough mirrors to get the full play by play and having private moments recorded for others to find is way too problematic. That monitor is a security screen connected to a motion sensor in my office. When I'm in here, it lets me see what's happening in my office. If someone pops in, I know before I head out."

"I suppose you don't want to saunter out of here in leather chaps and butt plug and scar the cleaning lady."

"Something like that."

The room grows quiet and I swallow. "This is me, Bear. It's not for everyone, but it's what I like."

"And you're like this with Jaxx and Calli?"

"Jaxx yes—very much. Calli... not yet. She and I are more like what you described before. We're in fuzzy handcuffs and vibrator territory. She's game but I'm taking things slow with her."

"But not with Jaxx?"

I chuckle. "I don't think Jaxx takes anything slow. Our jaguar is a wildcat."

Brant's lips curl in a seductive smile. "In all the best possible ways."

"Agreed."

When we both fall silent, that nervousness inches back. "If you're not interested... if it's too much—"

Brant raises a hand and strides across the room with full swagger. "I'm one hundy percent interested. I'm just not sure where to begin."

I don't want him to feel overwhelmed. It's one of the reasons I left the lights off. "You mentioned something about giving great head and easing the stress of my day. We could start there."

I walk over to the padded bench facing the glass wall between us and the city. There's a thick kneeling mat on the floor in front of it and I sit and spread my knees.

"Come here. Kneel on the mat and let me kiss you."

He surprises me by complying so quickly. Yes, he's beta and will submit to my alpha in most instances, but I didn't push my dominance. He came because he wanted to.

His hips are broad between my thighs and I run my hands from his shoulders across his collarbones and grip his neck. Touching him helps. Our mating bond kicks in the moment any of us touch one another. It's grounding.

"Thanks for your help tonight," I say, needing to say something so he doesn't think this is all about sex and stepping up to the bonding. "I enjoy working with you."

"Surprising as it is, we make a pretty good team."

I slide my fingers into the long, brown waves of his hair like I did in the restaurant. Was my body's response just me proving a point or because Carina was watching?

Fuck, I hope not.

I lean forward and close the distance between our mouths. The moment our lips meet and his bear growls, my senses pick up right where we left off at the restaurant.

The scent of the other three on his skin, the rumble of his bear's growl, my need to let him in and make our quint whole.

He's gained confidence since the restaurant.

Brant grips my jaw with one hand and reaches between us to stroke my cock with his other. "I'm fucking dying to tongue your cock piercing."

I chuckle and ease back against the angled backrest.

"Have at it, Bear. Who am I to deny a man his desire." With a firm hand, I pull his head into my lap.

His lips part over my crown and he sucks me deep into his throat. The suction isn't gentle. Which suits me perfectly. I grip a fistful of his curls and gently pump into his mouth.

It's torture to hold back.

I'll gain power over him eventually but I don't want to take his control until we build up a level of trust. "As rough as you like. Yeah... that's good."

Brant's right. He *does* give great head.

Once he gets rocking, I stretch my arms open over the back of the bench and watch the image of us in the mirrored ceiling. Fuck, that cranks me up.

I grip a fistful of his silky mop and grind him down on my cock. He's got a grip on the base of my shaft and is guiding his head up and down the ridges, lollipoping me like he's fucking obsessed.

When his free hand shifts between my legs, he twists my sac and my abdominals quake.

My release is building in my balls, the tingle of cum pushing hard against his kneading fingers. I get back to studying our image again and yeah, this is way hotter than any of the meaningless fucks of my pre-mating days.

This big, muscle-bound male, this guy sucking me hard while I fuck his mouth... this is my mate.

"I'm thirsty, avian. Come in my mouth." The hoarse catch in his timbre brings on a rush of urgency.

I grip his hair tighter. "I can take this all night long. What's your rush?"

The growl of his bear vibrates against my cock. "I want to be tied and fucked. I want to fuck you. I want it all. This is just the appetizer... so amuse my bouche, motherfucker."

I laugh but I'm close. My abs are tightening and I curl my hips. "Then suck me like you mean it, Bear. I'm about to mark you inside and out."

My hips lock and I grunt as the rush of hot cum releases. Brant's on it. Sucking and swallowing with a fervor that proves just how thirsty he is. "Every drop, Bear."

I close my eyes as another wave hits and I go off again. Fuck, it feels good. How did I ever win this lottery?

When the sucking stops, Brant straightens and looms over me. He claims my mouth and he tastes of cum and sorority drinks. "Where do you want me?"

"Do you have any concerns or triggers I need to know about?"

"Nope."

"And you're game for anything?"

"Yep."

I chuckle. "Then it's the cross for you."

"I take it you mean the giant wood and iron X."

"That's the one."

He closes the distance and eyes it up and down. "Okay, how do we do this?"

I chuckle. "It's not rocket science, Bear. Hands up and buckled. Feet spread and buckled. Voila, you're a giant X."

His grin is far too funny. "And you're going to fuck with me, right? Do your Dom thing and whip me and shit?"

We're chest to chest and I roll my eyes. "We're not playing naughty nurse here, Brant. Half the arousal is the mindset. Settle in, lock down your horny twelve-year-old and get ready to be fucked like never before."

Brant's chest bounces with amusement and rubs my nipple rings. "Sir, yes sir."

I buckle his wrists and then take a knee to lock his ankles. The position puts me at eye-level to his cock.

"While you're down there," Brant says, swaying his hips.

I chuckle and shake my head. "You can't help yourself, can you?"

Standing in front of the equipment board, I select a few things I think he might like. The mask is an easy one. I want him to settle down and start focusing on his physical sensations.

The visuals of the dungeon seem to be overloading him. The flogger with eighteen-inch leather tassels will give a sexy sting. Then, when I pivot the cross so he's horizontal, I have spicy cinnamon lube and a few other things in mind.

"Okay, Brant. Let the games begin."

CHAPTER SEVEN

Kotah

Calli comes apart on the third round of Jaxx's new mate game, Run, Hunt, Fuck. It's an inspired game and I've enjoyed my part in tracking the scent of her arousal through the halls. Now, hours in, most of the house smells like the two of them. Jaxx is in fine form tonight. He has pleasured Calli orally on the deck, on her knees bent over the coffee table, pressed against the window of the master, and now on the kitchen table.

"Mercy," she gasps. "My poor hoohaw is dripping wet and my nipples are throbbing."

Jaxx laughs. "I can't help how much I want you. It's your fault really."

"My fault? How do you figure?"

"Because you make me cum so hard I swear I'm a god and the sound of your feminine cries fills my soul. How's a male to turn away from that? Besides, we didn't get any trainin' in today, so it's my duty as your guardian to work you out to build up your stamina."

She barks a laugh. "I see. So then, does the training continue?"

"You bet your perky ass it does. Five. Four..."

"Wait. May I have a turn?" I rise to two feet as my wolf finally releases his hold on me. Calli and Jaxx break apart and the sheer joy in their expressions fills my heart. "May I get in on this action?"

"Hells yes you can, Wolf." Jaxx wraps his arms around me and hugs me tight. When he pulls back, he drops to his knees and tugs my sweatpants to the floor. He's got me in his mouth and sucking me stiff before I know what hits me.

Calli sits up on the table and I bend to kiss her. Her lips are gentle and loving and filled with tenderness. "Welcome back, sweetie. I love you."

"I love you too, *Chigua*."

"So," Jaxx says. "New game. It's called worship our wolf. It's played right here and ends when our wolf has cum to the point of exhaustion and begs for mercy."

Calli bites her lip. "Oh, I like this game already. I get to be the predator for a change instead of the prey."

"Now to lube you up and start the party," Jaxx says.

Calli reclines onto her back and opens her legs. "And as it happens I'm currently soaked and dripping. Might as well put those juices to work."

"Reuse. Recycle. Good thinking, kitten."

I chuckle at the two of them. "And what do I have to look forward to in this game of yours?"

Jaxx reaches around my hip and strokes me a couple of times. "Calli stays right where she is. Her legs are likely still quivering from our game."

"They are, thank you."

"You're welcome." He blows her a kiss and then turns back to me. "Kotah, you bury your cock in her heat and I'll fuck you slow and dirty from behind. Does that work for everyone?"

I swallow and nod. "Yes, please."

From where they moved the table next to the breakfast bar, Calli can lay on her back and prop her feet on the counter. Jaxx swipes his fingers through the glistening moisture seeping out of her core and cups his hand.

With a gentle nudge, we shift spots and I take the man-in-the-middle position. From behind me he wraps me in a tight embrace and kisses my cheek. "Welcome back, Wolf. We love you."

I meet Calli's smile and lean over her chest to kiss her. "I love you both."

Bent forward as I am, Jaxx takes the hint and starts priming. There's no self-consciousness when I'm with these two. The three of us have spent the most time together and we know anything goes.

I hold my cock and play in the folds of her core. Even with Jaxx swiping moisture to slick my backside, she's still creamy and wet. I slide into Calli's heat and exhale. The succulence of her cream and Jaxx's cum mixed with the scent of our arousal is too perfect.

I grip Calli's hips, make a couple of languid pumps of in and out, and then I drop forward and hug her tight. The moment I stop moving, Jaxx takes his cue and presses the tip of his cock right where I want him.

"My girls missed you, sweet prince."

I push up onto the palm of my hands and suckle one of the heaving mounds while fondling the other.

I love Calli's breasts.

"How you doin', Wolf?" Jaxx asks.

"Better now." I go back to sucking on Calli and she groans. Her back arches and she thrusts into my mouth.

Yeah. Much better now.

It doesn't take long for Jaxx to build up to a sensuous pull and push. My insides keen with sensation and my cock pulses inside Calli.

"More?" Jaxx asks.

"Much more," I growl a rush of emotion hitting me. "I need... I was..." I drop my forehead against Calli's sternum and she hugs me tight.

"Do you need to stop, sugar?"

I shake my head and push up. "No. Don't stop. I felt adrift all day. I want to connect."

"We've got you, buddy," Jaxx says. "Just check out and let us show you the love."

And with that, I do.

I hug Calli tight and suck her nipple into my mouth, soaking in the penetration of Jaxx's cock taking me from behind. How he can still be so hard after fucking Calli for the past couple of hours amazes me.

Then again, Jaxx is living, breathing passion.

We continue like that, Jaxx and I standing between Calli's legs, him hammering into me from behind and the force of his thrusts fucking me into Calli.

It's a glorious sensation. When his purr rumbles over us, Calli groans, and her womb clenches my cock.

I close my eyes and relish how her muscles milk me. Tugging and squeezing with every thrust.

"I love you, Kotah," Jaxx says, his voice strained. "Don't you ever forget it. And if your wolf steps in the way again, remind him how much I ache for you."

I brace my hands against the table and push back. "Show me how much."

The roar of Jaxx's jaguar slices the air.

It's not a sound he makes often but it holds all the power of his wild side. His fingers tighten against my hips with bruising force and he strikes a thundering pace. With each slam home, another wave of sensation singes my balls.

I ache too, my sac tightening, ready to release. "I'm close Jaxx. So, close."

I don't know how, but his cock swells inside me and feels bigger. He's lost all control and I lock my elbows to brace myself and keep from crushing Calli.

I needn't worry. She's not suffering. Our phoenix is heating up. Her eyes are closed, her breath catching. "Oh... yes."

She shatters and my mind spins. Her hips buck wild beneath me and I pin her down. My breath catches and my hips slam forward and lock. I let off a long, throaty howl.

My abs clench and burn as streams of cum fill my mate. The scent of my juices mix with theirs and all is right in my world. It didn't sit right with me—that only the two of them were blended when three of us were here.

Now, we're complete.

My arms are rubber and quiver as I lay my cheek on Calli's heaving chest and press back into Jaxx's thrusts.

"Mark me Jaxx. Claim what's yours."

I can barely stay upright as Jaxx's orgasm breaks free. His hips pitch forward in a final, solid thrust. "You *are* mine."

I smile at his loss of control. Yeah.

And they are mine, too.

Hawk

I've lost track of how many times Brant has come for me. His giddy-schoolboy mindset dissolved around the third orgasm and that was almost two hours ago when I moved him from the cross to tie him on the bed. Things I've learned about our bear. He enjoys the sting of a leather flogger on his ass... hot wax anywhere near his sac has him shooting streams of ropey cream... and I fucking love the taste of him.

I don't know what the chemical synergy of his cock in my mouth is, but it's like the succulence of the rarest vintage for me. I get off when it coats my tongue and warms the icy pit of my belly.

Oh, and one other thing I learned. When I push him for hours, his bear ascends and he gets really fucking rough.

"Again," I command.

His bear growls and it's not the playful rumble we're used to hearing. This is his wildling side pacing near the surface. He wants sex—actual intercourse—and I've deprived him. Partly to test his limits and partly to build the suspense.

My hand is wrapped around his cock and I'm jacking him off for the umpteenth time. His responsiveness is amazing and his beta instincts are well conditioned to my command by now. "Come for me this last time and then I'll release you."

"I won't be in control," he breathes, sweat dripping down his face. "My bear will come at you hard."

"I'm ready." More than ready.

With Jaxx, I let him take the lead. As a dom, he's fun and getting edgier. But with Brant, I'm not a sub. I'm his dom.

He's definitely going to come at me hard. His eyes are gold with his bear and his pulse is racing.

"Safeword?"

"Hydrogen."

"Ready?" He nods and I bend over his cream-slick cock. "One more taste and then we fuck."

When my mouth slides over his swollen tip and down his steel shaft, his hips convulse and I start to swallow. Brant's essence tastes like raw power. It hits my tongue and I groan and suck and swallow.

As much as I'd like to suck him dry, I don't.

I leave him drenched in cream and grab the bottle of lube. Cum is great in a pinch but for this, we both need the right supplies for the job. I lube him up, cock and ass, and then tend to myself. To start us off, I straddle his hips and impale myself on his cock.

Brant lets off a breathy curse as I grip his broad muscled chest. Rising up and slamming back down, I work in the moisture of lubrication. When that's done, I dismount and shift down the bed a bit to kneel between his thighs.

"Knees up."

"Fuck that. I want my cock back inside you."

"We'll see how well you listen. Knees up."

He lifts his knees and I push his thighs open wider. With all the play and lube, my cock pushes inside him with smooth and sexy efficiency. I close my eyes and feel that glorious rush of penetration, thrust, and glide.

It's a shame to stop but I've pushed him far enough. We're both primed for whatever happens. With that in mind, I remove his mask, the buckles on his ankle restraints, and then the buckle holding his wrists tied together over his head.

The moment he's free, he lifts me off the bed and flips me onto my belly. I elbow him off and fight to top him. The challenge is well received and for the next few minutes, we're a frantic scramble of fighting wills and the sheer carnal strength of an alpha wanting to be dom and a stubborn, horny bear wanting his way.

It's perfect. I get a fist to the face and my head snaps to the side. The world spins in a blur and I'm face down in the sheets. He impales me hard and fast and I grunt at the penetration. "I'll give you five minutes and then it's game on again and we battle for position."

I check the digital clock on the wall and press my head into the silk. Jaxx was so right about the beauty of sex with men. I would never let a female flip me on my knees and fuck me, but with Brant, a beta, and my mate, he understands I'm allowing him to fill me.

In essence, I'm topping him from the bottom.

"Fuck your ass is tight," Brant grunts, his breath coming in short bursts. "You feel so good."

"Three minutes, Bear. Then I fuck you."

He barks a laugh. "After hours of torture, my bear is fucking you non-stop for a week."

"You loved every minute," I say, getting face-planted into the mattress by the sheer force of Brant's bear.

"Abso-fucking-lutely."

I close my eyes and live in the moment. Yes, my business life is under attack, but right now, things are good. I watch the number on the clock. When it flips, I elbow Brant in the side of the head, roll free, and mount Brant from behind.

With him flat on the mattress, I push inside him again and reach under his pelvis to grip his cock. "Let me fuck you now, Bear. Let the mating bond lock."

The fight he was about to mount dissolves and the tension in his muscles relax. With the mating bond in mind, I focus on how good it feels to connect with Brant. He's more than a fun ride, he's smart and brave and devoted to Calli and our quint.

The tremendous yearning I feel at the closeness of him over-whelms. I drop my mouth to his shoulder and bite his flesh. His bear grumbles and at the next press of my hips energy explodes between us.

I groan, still biting, still filling him and receding in long, languid strokes. Our mating bond takes hold and courses between us, swirling from my system to his and back again. As before, with Jaxx and Calli, the connection links us.

We two are now one. We are together, complete.

The fire of Calli's phoenix licks over my skin and I feel her with us. Jaxx is here too. My mates.

Brant's feeling it too. He groans, but not from pain.

He thrusts his hips into my palm, grinding and humping the mattress. My need to claim him increases and burns inside me. It's torture. Succulent. Erotic torture.

"Mine," I pant, my hips faltering with the building of my release. "Say it. You're mine."

Brant throws his head back and grunts. "Fuuuck."

He's thrusting into the sheets, his ass clenching and squeezing me beyond my control. "I'm yours. I'm so, fucking yours. I've never been this turned on."

My release erupts in a fiery blast and I collapse on his back, marking him inside and out, with my bite, my hand, my mating mark. When I have the strength to roll off him, I flop onto the bed beside him and try to get reacquainted with breathing. The loss of heat makes me shiver and I lay flat on my back to cool off.

It is no wonder Calli passed out in the early days. What we are—the five of us together—is wild and overwhelming.

Brant groans beside me, lying flat out. "I may have just suffered a coronary."

"Well, I'm no help to you. I can't move a muscle."

"Then I'll have to die a happy man."

CHAPTER EIGHT

Hawk

A squeeze of my arm wakes me from a deep sleep. I blink and look into Brant's eyes. He presses a finger against his lips and I nod in understanding. With the key to the handcuffs I had him lock me in when we went to bed, he frees my hands. What's got him so tense? When I'm free, he points up at the monitor in the corner.

The motion sensor in my office is triggered and showing me an empty room.

"Who was in there?"

Brant looks like he has something to say, but holds off.

"It's okay. I made this room soundproof for obvious reasons. What did you see?"

"There was a tall guy, blond hair, pointy nose. He was at your desk with the ebony-haired woman I'm assuming is your assistant Jayne. They were fussing with each other. It seemed to me she was pissed."

"Pissed about our little video maybe?"

"Maybe."

I hop off the bed and grab the towel from the table. Bare-footing it out to my office, I wrap the scrap of terry around my hips. The lights are still off and if Brant hadn't told me they were just here, I never would have known. "Everything looks undisturbed. What exactly did they touch?"

"The guy was at your computer. The female stood on the opposite side of the desk with her arms crossed. Whatever they were arguing about, it wasn't a friendly disagreement."

"Maybe our video caused a stir in the rank of traitors."

"Do you think you know who the guy was?"

"Blond guy with a straight nose and arguing with Jayne? Yeah. That's Hunter."

"Your Director of Operations."

"Yep."

"Do you think they're in on it together?"

"I don't know but it's a little damning that they were snooping in my office at four o'clock in the morning on the day I retake control of my life. What did they touch exactly?"

Brant opens his mouth to tell me and the door to my office opens again.

Jayne stops dead in her tracks and her expression drops. "Oh… you're here."

"My office. The building still has my name on it… or has that been changed too? You and Hunter have been busy little beavers."

Her expression falls. "It's not what you think."

I drop the towel and stride back to my dungeon to grab my pants. "It's not what I *wanted* to believe but the evidence speaks for itself. We caught you here. The monitor activated the moment you and Hunter came snooping."

"Then if you were watching on the monitor, you know I wasn't helping him. He's twisting things to make it look like you're a traitor to the fae and his fucking around shines me in the light of the most likely suspect. You know me better."

"I thought I did." I button my slacks and sling on my shirt. "I didn't want to believe it but yeah, 'most likely suspect' is what I came up with too."

The fury and betrayal in her eyes stab me right in the gut. "After our years taking over the world together. Do you honestly think I'd do this?"

"You were pissed about Calli and the quint," Brant says. "Nothing more dangerous than a woman scorned."

She rolls her eyes. "Listen, moose. You look good naked and are probably still a little light-headed from a night with Barron in the dungeon, but let me lay something out for you. I love this company and whether or not he and I are fucking, I know he's the best person to keep FCO on track. We see the fae world in the same light—that's why we work well together. You and your lunatic female can have his cock—there are plenty more—but this company means more to me than a lifetime of orgasms."

"That's nice to hear." I finish buttoning my shirt and smile. "But if you call Calli a lunatic again, I snap your fucking neck. Other than that, I think you made your point."

She rolls her eyes and flicks her manicured fingers at me. "We'll agree to disagree on the mental state of your mate."

Brant advances, his frame growing more intimidating as his muscles grow rigid. "And we agree that your neck is a twig if you mouth off about her ever again."

Jayne has the good sense to look afraid. "Agreed. I shall speak nothing but saccharine-sweet praise when it comes to our phoenix. Surely the universe sees something in her I don't."

I finish tucking in my shirt and latch my belt. "Tell me what the hell has been going on here."

"I can't," Jayne says. "Not because I don't want to. I can't..." her words cut off and she growls.

I feel the tingle of magic in the air. She grimaces and takes a step back. "I *am* sorry, Hawk. I've tried to catch your attention but my hands are tied."

"How is Victor?"

Jayne flashes me a look of utter relief. "Surrounded by powerful people."

"Send him my regards."

"Thank you."

She turns to leave and my mind is whirling through information. "Jayne?"

"Yes?"

"How much time do we have until the Eddison deal is finalized?"

The side of her mouth turns up in a crooked smile. "It won't be long now. Days... a week or two at most."

"Alright. I'll take it from here."

She nods. "Understood."

When it's just Brant and me in the office once more, he turns to me. "What the hell was that about? What's the Eddison deal?"

I round my desk and wake up my computer. "The Eddison deal was something I was considering when I first took Jayne under my wing and promoted her as my assistant. I was so sure it was a money-making winner, I missed a few financial cues that the company was dealing in illegal fae magic. Jayne was a young startup, looking to impress me and dug her heels in. Her father, Victor, is an empath and it made him a king in business. Jayne shares his gift and instincts."

"And she saved you from making a big mistake?"

"She saved FCO from total destruction. The Eddison deal would've brought down the whole house of cards."

"So when you asked how long we have until the Eddison deal is finalized..."

"Yeah, we haven't got long before the world around us crashes to the ground."

~

Calli

Lukas is waiting at the kitchen table for us first thing in the morning. And, for once, Jaxx and I are showered and dressed and ready for guests. That's a win. Yay team. Kotah flipped into his wolf and has gone for a morning run.

"Good morning," I say, as Jaxx and I head straight for the coffee machine. It's hot and ready. Another win. We're killing it this morning. "Do I have you to thank as our brewmaster this morning?"

"I just pushed the button. I thought the smell might lure you down."

Jaxx pulls out the egg carton and milk and starts puttering at the stove. "Omelet?"

Lukas waves that off. "I'm good. Your mother fed me and I'm stuffed."

I pour two steaming cups and take them to the counter where Jaxx has the milk. "Well, thank you for the java lure. I'm grateful to not have to wait."

Jaxx pulls out a wedge of ham and a block of cheese. "So if not my cookin', what brings you by so early?"

Lukas points to the laptop Hawk gave me on the table. "Check your inbox, Calli. I sent you a video you should see. It seems Barron and Brant were busy last night."

I snort and look at Jaxx. We know just how busy he and Brant were last night but... a video? That doesn't seem like their style. And why would Lukas have it?

I set down my cup of java and sign in. And yep. there is indeed a video in my inbox from CFO head office. As the file loads, Jaxx pulls up a chair beside me and sips at his mug.

The image opens with Hawk looking very corporate, sitting in a leather chair with a fancy lamp beside him.

"Good evening everyone,

My name is Hawk Barron. Many of you know me as one of the

chosen Guardians of the Phoenix. What you might not know is that I am also the Owner/Operator of the Fae Concealment Office, and am the civilian representative of Fae and Monster Rights for the Fae Council.

It has come to my attention over the past weeks that a villainous faction is working behind the scenes in my company, the Fae Palace, and the Fae Council to undermine the opening of the Portal Gate.

When I say villainous, I want you to understand, it is not hyperbole. My mates and I have had our helicopter sabotaged, our vehicle run off the road, and have been set upon by militia armed with automatic weapons and rocket launchers. Some of you will remember the attack at the Bastion last month. All four of my mates were in that cabin when it exploded.

Even before we were aware of this plot and working to track down those responsible, the poison was spreading. Empowered teenagers were kidnapped and held hostage, human women and illegal guns were sold... the list is as extensive as it is deplorable.

It has been made to look like I am behind it, but that couldn't be further from the truth. The group hiding in the shadows call their leader the Black Knight. Well, I'm here to tell them that there are no more shadows. I'm shining a light on you.

The Phoenix rose for a reason. The Portal Gate will be opened. And the Black Knight and his or her followers will be crushed.

This morning, Nakotah Northwood, your Fae Prime in Waiting survived an assassination attempt. I'm pleased to say he's standing strong and fighting mad as are we all. Until this plot is stopped, I'm invoking a halt on all calls-to-action, pending changes, and motions put before the Fae Prime's office, the Fae Council, and the FCO. Consider our governing bodies on a time-out until the weeds are pulled.

So, Black Knight, it's on. There will be no closures of fae reservations, no transfers of deeds, no fucking with our lives. If you want to come at me, grow some fucking balls and come at me head-on. The *fact you chose a game of chess proves what a pathetic bunch of pussies you are.*

To you, the bystanders of all this. If you witness activity unbecoming our community or have seen or heard something that threatens our people, call the FCO head office. Ask the switchboard for the Guardians of the Fae Realms line and someone from my team will hear your concerns.

I am truly sorry for anyone who has been negatively impacted by these cowards. Your representatives will do everything in our power to make it right.

Thank you, and good night."

I blink and look up at Lukas. "So, that happened."

Lukas chuckles. "It was a bold move to throw it into the public eye. But that's our Barron. If you stab him you better make damn sure he's dead or else he'll get up and make you wish you were."

I nod. "Into the city, I take it?"

"Yep. Finish your omelets. I'll be back in twenty to take the three of you in."

CHAPTER NINE

Calli

Lukas calls the helicopter back to Montclair and takes me, Jaxx, and Kotah to Manhattan to join our mates. Kotah's back in wolf form and I'm not sure why. Jaxx and I had a wonderful session with him in the kitchen and then moved upstairs to the bed to slow things down for some sensual loving. Everything was good until we felt the twang of Brant and Hawk's mating bond activate.

Then Kotah withdrew.

I believe his wolf taking over yesterday was to protect him from physical danger. I'm not sure what it's about today.

When we get close, Lukas slows and pulls into the curb lane. "Do you want to be dropped at the road and go in through the main entrance or parking garage and up?"

Jaxx looks at me and then shrugs. "Let's keep a low profile until we talk to Hawk about what they found last night. No sense tipping our hand to the conspirators that the Phoenix Quint is descending if they haven't already clued in."

Lukas hits the indicator and drives us in the side of the building and down a concrete ramp.

"Have you spoken to him this morning?" I ask.

Lukas navigates the underground parking and takes one of three spots right next to the elevator. "Several times. He and Brant spoke with Jayne. He officially removed her from the list of traitors. He believes she's being coerced into compliance but has been trying to warn him for weeks, he simply was too preoccupied to notice."

"I hate that bitch."

Jaxx chuckles. "Easy, kitten. Your first encounter stands as one of our most memorable moments, but perhaps you both got off on the wrong foot. Hawk's a keen judge of character. If he knows what he knows and still values her, there has to be a reason." He catches something in my expression and shakes his head. "And that reason has nothin' to do with residual affection for her. He loves us now."

Kotah's wolf chuffs beside me and he lifts his lips, exposing his canines.

Yep. it's going to be another cranky wolf day.

Lukas waits until we're all out of the truck and then locks up. The beep of the alarm echoes against the hard surfaces of the parking garage. It's close to nine and most of the spots are filled for the day.

He pockets his keys, steps into the elevator kiosk, and bypasses the steel doors of the public elevators. Opening a door to the right, he stops before a smaller, black metal door.

"This is the executive elevator," he says, pressing his palm on a scanner. When the device reads his palm, it flashes his name and allows us entrance.

"Fancy," Jaxx says. "It's fun sleepin' with the boss."

The elevator car thumps and bumps as it settles into place and when the doors open, we're on our way.

Checking his phone, Lukas punches two floors. "Jaxx, he asks that you go to Legal on eighteen. Brant's there working with Penny from Property Rights and a junior clerk tracking down anything the Black Knight might have fucked with. Calli and Kotah, I'm to escort you two up to his office on thirty and warn you that Jayne is there and he's sorry she upsets you but he needs her at the moment and would appreciate you not burning down his building."

"I hate that bitch."

Jaxx chuckles. "You may have mentioned that once or twice."

When the elevator doors open, Jaxx kisses my temple and steps onto the floor. Kotah trots off at his heel.

"Aren't you supposed to come with me, Wolf?"

Kotah exposes his canines and growls.

I flash him my palms. "Or not. Okay, we'll regroup later. Love you boys, good luck."

The door closes and we continue to rise. What the hell is going on with Kotah? "Hey, Lukas?"

Hawk's right-hand man finishes with his phone and slides it in his pocket. "Yes? Something you need?"

"Nope." I step forward and hug him. He stiffens like a plank of hardwood and I smile. He's about as comfortable with random physical affection as Hawk was in the beginning. I put him out of his misery quickly and step back. "Thank you. I want to say you're appreciated. Your dedication and skill don't go unnoticed. We think you rock."

He stretches his neck and swipes his tongue across his lips. "You're welcome. I… think you are all worth the effort."

The elevator doors open. He's still discombobulated and I chuckle. No wonder he and Hawk get along so well. Neither of them is into touchy-feely. With a firm hand on my lower back, Lukas guides me through the upper floor of the Fae Concealment Office headquarters.

We pass the open door of the office beside Hawk's and I catch a glance of Jayne. She's sitting with her ankles crossed at her glass desk, looking sleek and powerful in her designer dress and her Louboutins. Bitch.

I admit, not all of my hatred and distrust of her comes from a place of reason. There is a part of me that recognizes that she is everything I'll never be: sophisticated, a corporate mogul, and the logical match for a man like Hawk Barron.

Our gazes meet as we pass and I flip her the bird.

She smiles and sends me the ocular version of the same message. Good. At least we know where we both stand.

"Hey, you're here." Hawk rises from his desk and I'm struck by him sitting there looking all professional CEO. He comes to greet me and I welcome the hug. "Where's Kotah? I wanted to see him and apologize about yesterday morning now that he's back."

"Was back," I correct. "He's wolfed up again."

"What? Why? Did something happen?"

I look over to Lukas and smile. "Do you mind if we have a moment?"

Lukas checks with Hawk and then dips his chin. "Not a problem. I have work at my desk. Let me know when you're ready to leave."

"Thank you, Lukas." Hawk waits until the door shuts and then sits on the end of his desk. "What's wrong? Is he still feeling the effects of the poison?"

"No. He said he felt better."

"Is his wolf still being protective of him? Coming out in the open like this? Maybe Manhattan was a bad idea."

"I think his wolf is being protective, but not from assassination." I squeeze his wrists and sigh. "I think his wolf is upset with you."

"Me? I would never hurt him."

The confusion and concern in Hawk's gaze warm my heart. He has come a long way. "Whatever's going on between you two, bit us in the ass last night. The three of us had a lovely welcome back love-in and then your bonding with Brant hit us. He muttered something about never being enough and flipped back to his wolf."

The pain in Hawk's expression tells me he knows exactly what this is about. He pushes off his desk and begins to pace.

"The two of you argued yesterday morning. You said he was angry and looking for a fight. What was that about?"

Hawk runs his hands over his face and then tips his head back. "Fuuuuck!"

I cross my arms. "Oh, Hawk. What did you do?"

His mouth tightens into a tight line. "Oh, so it's me, is it? I'm the one causing the fight?"

I draw a deep breath and unclench my fists. "I'm sorry. Kotah is the sweetest and most patient man I've ever met. It hurts me that he's hurting. I didn't mean to come at you with my finger-wagging but if he's the one feeling hurt then something happened."

Hawk strides over to the window and stares out at the city. "He said I didn't accept him as a mate because he'll never be enough for me. He said you and Jaxx were the mates I chose and he and Brant were the throwaways."

"And then you mated Brant."

He hangs his head and exhales. "I thought... fuck, I'm trying so hard to make everyone happy."

I uncross my arms and hug him from behind. "I know. I'm sorry I snapped. If it's any consolation, Jaxx and I think you're doing great. And, given the lust vibrating over the mating bond last night, Brant is warming up to you too."

He turns to face me and pulls me into his chest. "I didn't mean to snub, Kotah. He's just so perfect. Of all of you, I'm afraid to fuck up with him the most."

"Have you told him that?"

"I was trying when he pretty much died in my arms."

I hug him tighter. "Okay. We'll figure that out. You do have feelings for him though, right? The pull of the mating bond is there? You could love him?"

Hawk huffs. "How could anyone *not* love him. He's a saint. A brilliant, sexy, well-mannered saint."

Yeah. True story.

We stand like that holding onto one another for a bit until Hawk finally straightens. "I have one more question."

"Yeah, what's that?"

"Why is Lukas's scent on you? Have you two got something hot and steamy going on the side?"

I burst out laughing. "Yeah, because I need another cock in the mix."

"Hey, just asking. He's got that buff, military soldier thing going for him."

"No doubt. He's a pleasure to look at, but no. I hugged him in the elevator and told him how much I appreciate everything he's done for us over the past months. No clandestine love affair."

"That's good. I'd hate to have to kill my best friend."

I reach up on my tiptoes and claim his mouth. "Your bestie can live another day. I'm only fooling around with four men at the moment."

Hawk chuckles and pulls me tight to his chest. "Well, as long as it's only four."

Jaxx

Kotah and I don't see Brant when we get off the elevator, so we head over to ask the closest person where we might find—

"Where is Penny?"

I follow the hostile voice to a tall, blond guy shooting

daggers around the room. "Come on, people. Penelope Fremont. I was told she's up here. Now, where is she?"

A timid-looking brunette stands in her cubical and points down the hall. "Penny's in conference room B with Dillan and a guest of—"

Angry blond stomps off, and Kotah and I follow suit. If Hawk wanted to stir up dust with his video announcement this morning, this guy might be part of the sandstorm.

The guy is booking it down the hall and Kotah and I have to jog to keep up. When he rips into the room, he stops in the doorway and thumbs over his shoulder. "Penny, I need to speak to you privately. It's urgent."

Kotah and I stop up the hall. The conference room has glass walls and I meet Brant's gaze. He's sitting behind a long table, glaring at the asshat between us.

"Penny. Now, please."

"Yes, sir."

The sweet thing looks like she might pee her panties and my cat takes offense to the intimidation. By the growl rumbling out of my wolf, I'd say Kotah feels the same way.

"What's your beef with Penny, Mr. Gable?" I ask.

He swings around and scowls. "Do I know you?"

"Not personally, but I've been lookin' at your mug for the past week on my office wall. And after the way you just spoke to the ladies in this office, I feel like I know you."

He turns to face me and I step in close. "Not so mouthy now, eh?"

"Fuck you."

He moves to pass me and I shift to block him. "Do not pass Go. Do not collect two hundred dollars. Now. What's your problem with Penny? What's so urgent that you forgot how to behave like a gentleman?"

"Who are you? You don't even work here."

"Answer his question, dickwad," Brant says, joining the testosterone party in the hall. "What's your beef with Penny?"

"That's company business and none of yours."

I turn to the lady in question. "What are you workin' on that Mr. Gable might be so worked up about this mornin', sweetheart?"

She shrugs. "Nothing. I've been working on the fae reservation closures full-time for three weeks. With Mr. Barron shutting that down, I have no current task outside of what we're doing here with the Guardians of the Fae Realms. Searching for areas of compromise and tracking the sources."

"Did you hear that, Mr. Gable? The lady sees no reason why you should need her attention."

Brant pushes forward. "Unless you *are* concerned about the closure of the fae reservations getting halted. Did you have something to do with that clusterfuck?"

He frowns. "Of course not. Everyone knows that was all Barron."

Brant and I chuckle and Kotah growls. "Everyone here knows it has nothing to do with Hawk Barron."

Blondie laughs. "Bullshit baffles. And after one stupid video, you believe him? He's saving his ass. He's as corrupt and dishonest as they come. Don't believe everything you hear boys." He looks around and can't see his opening to leave. That's because there isn't one.

His hand shoots out and grabs my throat.

Before he has time to squeeze, our wolf launches.

The scream of horror makes me giggle. "I've heard of actions bitin' someone in the ass, but wow... biting you in the nut sac must be so much worse."

Hunter drops to the ground, his feet flailing as he tries to wriggle away like the backsliding worm he is. Kotah still has a solid hold of the man's junk and stalks him step by step.

"Get your mutt off me. I'll fucking sue you bastards. Do you have any idea who my father is?"

Kotah flips out of wolf and stands tall. He wipes the blood from his mouth and then taps the purple Fae Prime tat on his cheek. "Do you have any idea who *my* father is?"

Hunter groans and rolls onto his knees. "You'll regret this. We'll make you pay."

~

Hawk

"We who?" I say, joining the guys down on eighteen. I look my Director of Operations up and down. He's sweating like a motherfucker and his crotch is bleeding. "Did something literally come back to bite you in the balls?"

"You're welcome," Kotah snaps.

I flash Kotah a warm smile and get back to Hunter. "Did you think we wouldn't put it together?"

He lists to the side, his shoulder catching on the wall to hold him up. "You haven't put anything together. I worked here under your nose for three years and you're as clueless now as you were then."

The dazed look of agony gives me my best chance of playing him against his boss. "If you say so. Or maybe I let you *think* that so I could keep an eye on you."

He chuckles. "Nice try."

"Do you think he doesn't know you're his brother?" Kotah snaps, a snarl in his voice. "Or half-brother I should say. Same father, different mothers."

It's a good thing Hunter is staring at Kotah because there's no hiding the shock from my expression. I draw a deep breath and compose myself. Before he looks back, I've got my mask of arrogance back in place.

Kotah's sense of smell as a wolf is incredible. If it's true… it explains so much. "So, Daddy Dearest wants to tear me to the ground, does he?"

Hunter chuffs. "Don't flatter yourself. You've been dead to him for twenty years. I came to see what all the hype was about. Let's say I'm underwhelmed."

I force a laugh, my head spinning. I widen my stance and fortify myself. I did *not* see this coming. "Our father's not the kind of man to forgive and forget. I thumbed my nose at him and made a life for myself. That's eating away at him, isn't it? That's why he made this so personal."

"There's nothing personal about you two. You're a narcissistic, twisted fuck."

Brant, Jaxx, and Kotah all rumble off a warning growl at the same time. The color in Hunter's face drains bone-white.

I smile. "Careful. I happen to be *their* narcissistic, twisted fuck and their wildling sides are a fuck ton more deadly than ours."

"He hates you, you know. You disgust him."

I chuckle. "And you sound like a petulant child spouting things you wish were true. So, who's your mother? One of our servants? The wife of a rival businessman? One of his regular Saturday night whores?"

That gets a rise out of him. "You don't know me. You know nothing about me."

I laugh at that. "If that man had anything to do with your upbringing and shaping you, I know everything I need to. The fact that you spied on me and plotted for three years proves you're a chip off the old man block. You could've told me the truth. I always wanted a brother."

"Bullshit. You don't do family."

"Bullshit," Brant snaps. "You didn't give him a chance."

"It's sad. If anyone on this planet understands where you're coming from, it's me. We could've been allies. You chose to be enemies. Lukas, show Hunter the door."

Lukas nods and grabs him by the arm. Brant meets my gaze and tips his head. I give him a nod. If he wants to play bouncer to my illegitimate baby brother, he's welcome to.

Kotah escorts Penny back into the conference room and closes the door.

Calli hugs me around the waist and Jaxx presses his forehead to my temple. "I'm sorry, Bastian. That was a shitty way to find out you have family you didn't know about."

Hearing him call me by my given name strengthens my soul. "I have all the family I need in you four."

Calli kisses my jaw. "Do you truly believe your father could be part of this?"

"Not part of it," I say, my throat tight with fury. "My father doesn't allow other players in his games. If Sabastian Barron Whitehouse Senior is involved in this clusterfuck, he *is* the Black Knight."

Calli squeezes me tighter and nuzzles my neck. "I get why he'd come after you—that's personal—but why come after us and try to keep me from opening the Portal Gate?"

I shrug and turn toward the elevators. "I don't know yet, but our answers—at least some of them—lie upstairs. We need to speak to Jayne…"

CHAPTER TEN

Hawk

"*D*id you know?" I lead the charge into Jayne's office and Calli and Jaxx follow close on my heels.

Jayne looks up from the open folder of reports she's highlighting. Her smile is intentionally obtuse and fuels my already bad temper. "I know a great many things, darling. Know what exactly?"

Before I'm dealing with another fireball incident, I nudge Calli sideways into Jaxx's arms. With a tilt of my head, I send the two of them over to sit in the chairs in the lounge area of the executive suite.

Jaxx settles into the oversized club chair and pulls Calli into his lap. For once, I don't think it's the jaguar attempting to get handsy. He's keeping her within his clutches to remain in control of her homicidal impulses.

Smart man.

"Don't do that," I say, pegging Jayne with a stern look. "Your days of calling me darling are over and you know it. Please don't jam me up on purpose. I want this to work and you're not making it easy."

Jayne rolls her eyes and sighs. "Where's your fighting spirit, Barron. You used to love to spat and spar."

"Now it's all I do. The world is coming at us from every angle. Fighting has lost its appeal. Believe it or not, I'm happiest now when I'm playing drinking games and laughing with my mates."

She studies my expression and some of the anger and hostility slips away. "I am glad you're happy. Truly. I'm over the insanity of it all and have taken a couple of lovers myself. Whether any of them hold interest in a month or two is still a mystery. You never know."

I chuckle. "I wish you well on that and please wish them luck from me."

She smiles and sits back in her chair. "So, back to your question. Did I know? Know what?"

"Did you know Hunter is my half-brother?"

She closes her eyes and smiles. "Recently I discovered a few... similarities between the two of you I never noticed before. I clued in, yes."

"How recently?"

"Once I started fucking him."

I frown. "That's disturbing. You're saying my half-brother fucks like me?"

"No. I'm saying that while spending time with Hunter in a more intimate setting, I noticed mannerisms and ticks that the two of you share. That strange way you use your fork... little sayings I've only ever heard you say... It was enough of an echo for me to take notice and have him investigated further. That's when my life went to shit."

"They have your father? Your comment about him being surrounded by powerful people. They've threatened you by threatening him."

She smiles and looks at the small, silver keys on her desk. Her intention is clear. After working so closely with her for over a decade, I can read her better than anyone on the planet. Not that I'd admit that to anyone.

Calli already wants to kill her.

I pick up the keys and walk over to unlock her file cabinet. Nothing out of the ordinary... except a manilla envelope with her name written in black ink on the front. I pull it out and she nods. I take the cue and open it up.

Taking the contents over to the desk, I spread out a dozen glossy shots of her father sitting in his wheelchair on a little bridge by the koi pond, sitting alone on a third-story balcony, him being fed his dinner in the community dining hall.

The message is clear. Whoever sent these can get to Victor Trenton. And, considering he's the one thing Jayne cares for above all else, the message would have been enough.

"When did this arrive?"

She moves her lips to answer me but stops. I feel the same sensation of magic tingling in the air that I felt before. "You're spelled to silence." She lets off a sigh and sits heavily in her chair. "You used to be far more observant. That took you weeks."

"They forced your compliance or they'll take it out on your father."

She tries to speak and frowns when her voice is cut off and the magic spikes.

"Okay, I get it. There are things you want to say but can't. I'm assuming this restriction also covers communicating in forms other than voice."

"Powerful people are efficient."

"I'll take that as a yes."

"Alright, so, you start fucking Hunter and you recognize we have some inherited quirks. You look into him further and figure out he hasn't disclosed everything and might have an ulterior motive for working his way up in my company."

"You have good instincts."

"Then you got too close to the truth and they bound your interference with magic and by dangling a threat over Victor."

The fire in her gaze tells me how much she despises being censored. "I tried to get your attention."

"And I didn't have my eye on the ball. Were you in trouble when you ambushed Calli at the palace? Was that a move to get my attention."

"Your attention, yes, but only because I was angry."

"And a bitch," Calli adds.

I look over to where she and Jaxx are sitting in the chair and Calli puts her hand over her mouth. "Oops, did I say that out loud? My mistake. Carry on."

When I get back to focusing on Jayne she's smiling. "She's not wrong. That was a bitch move."

"Moving past that…" I say, trying to get past the name-calling. "I'm sorry my family dysfunction impacted you and your father. It's not something I would have allowed had I known."

"Understood."

Jaxx moves to stand beside me and squeezes my shoulder. "May I ask somethin'?"

I gesture for him to take the stage.

"Does us figurin' out Hunter's identity and outin' him put you or your father in any immediate danger?"

The answer is in her gaze.

I turn and curse. "Spitfire, call Lukas, and have him send a security team to secure Victor Trenton. I want him moved to my penthouse and a twenty-four-hour guard and nurse there at all times."

She nods and steps into the hall. "Got it."

Jaxx looks at the images of Jayne's father and frowns. "Have you seen or spoken to Hawk's father or have you only dealt with Hunter?"

Jayne smiles but doesn't say anything.

I curse. "Okay, this spell is pissing me off."

"Really? Pissing *you* off?"

Jaxx frowns. "We need Lukas to—"

My phone vibrates in my pocket and I pull it free.

"What's the matter?" Jaxx asks, leaning over to read the screen. "Who is it?"

"It's an internal FCO line." I accept the call and answer. "Barron."

"Mr. Barron, sir?" someone says in barely a whisper.

I cover my ear to hear better. "Hello?"

"A dozen men with guns coming your way."

"Mallory?" I snap my fingers and point at the door. Jaxx gets the point and rushes to pull Calli in from the hall. "Thank you, Mallory. Get out of the building."

I end the call and my survival instincts kick in. "Jaxx pull the alarm. We've got company coming and they're heavily armed. Calli text Brant and Kotah. They need to haul ass up here. Now."

I point to Jayne. "Take the dumbwaiter and get out. Go to my penthouse and wait for your father. Go."

Jayne kicks off her shoes and slips on her trainers she keeps for the workout room. With her purse strap slung over her shoulder, she rushes toward the door. "You need to live to kick their asses, Barron. Seriously. Come with me."

"Right behind you. I won't leave without my mates." I wave for her to get going. "Be safe."

Kotah

103

My cell goes off at the same moment the emergency siren starts chiming. I pull the phone from my pocket and frown. *Company coming. Get to us. Top floor.* I read the text at the same time Brant reads his.

"Penny," I say, grabbing the files we've put together. "Black Knight men are coming. We need to get to Hawk and the others on the top floor."

She sees I'm struggling to find somewhere to put the files and dumps out her computer bag. "Take this. No offense, Majesty, but I'm safer *not* being with you. I'll be fine. I'll evacuate with everyone else and be fine."

I shove the files into her bag and sling it over my shoulder. "Thank you for your help and good luck."

"You too." Penny opens the door to the stairwell and starts her way down in the flood of traffic.

Brant and I start our way up.

"To the right, people," Brant shouts. "Get to the fucking right." When a bear bellows in a stairwell, you better believe people listen.

"The good news is," I say, pushing past a cluster of scared employees, "the alarm should lock down the elevators, so anyone coming after us will have the same problem."

Gunfire lights off above us and the stairwell erupts in a frantic echo of screaming.

Brant curses. "Unless they also drop a fucking helicopter onto the roof."

His bear lets off a roar and he plays the part of an offensive lineman as the two of us round the landing on the twenty-third floor. "What floor is the top?"

"No idea," I say tucking in behind him as we run. "The one where the stairs stop."

Brant grumbles, the sound part chuckle and part growl. "No one likes a smart ass, Wolf."

"You do."

The next grumble is definitely laughter. "Okay, you got me there."

By the time we get to the twenty-fifth floor, everyone seems to have evacuated and we've got clear sailing straight to the top. The roar of Jaxx's jaguar has my wolf rushing forward. My mates are in trouble. I need to get there.

Brant feels the same way because he's become a wildling juggernaut and is barreling forward like a tank. Or like an infuriated grizzly is likely closer to the truth.

The low-pitched *tat-a-tat-a-tat* is the sound of automatic weapons. The *crack, crack, crack* sound is Hawk's twin Sigs unloading. Thank the Powers he's always so prepared.

When we round the landing on the thirtieth floor, Brant grabs the handle and rips the door right off the hinges. Holding it in front of us like a shield he turns left and bolts down the hall.

For a moment, I wonder how he knows where to go.

Right. He spent the night here with Hawk.

My wolf howls, but I don't have time to think about how much that hurt me, right now.

Brant is bowling men down with the steel door and I grab a few of their guns as we run past. I'd prefer to fight in wolf form, but we need these files and I imagine Calli's going to be too hot to handle them.

If I can get them to Hawk, I can shift. He prefers to fight as a man. We get to the end of the hall and break into the melee already in progress.

Jaxx is snarling and clawing at a downed man. The jaguar's shoulder is bleeding but it's not bad enough that he's nursing it. Calli is a woman aflame and is human-torching her way forward. The hostiles seem to have learned that bullets melt before they damage her and they're pretty much screwed.

Sucks to be you, assholes.

Brant gets us into the room proper and swings the metal

door like a frisbee. The torn steel catches one of the attackers in the neck and his head severs and spins across the office whipping blood like a pinwheel. The body of the guy falls to the carpet not far from where Hawk is crouched behind the cover of his bar. He hears the thud and pops up, guns aimed.

"Shit. I almost shot you."

I look around. "Is that it? Are we squared away?"

Hawk shakes his head. "No. That's just the roof crowd. There's a ground crew coming too."

"I vote we leave before they get here," Brant says.

"You've got my vote," Jaxx says, prodding the wound on his shoulder.

"I'm good to stay and fry people," Calli says.

Hawk rolls his eyes. "So that's four for getting out while the getting's good and one for the last stand at the Alamo."

Calli's flame is holding strong and she's so, incredibly beautiful when she's fired up. "Or maybe it's *Die Hard* and this is our Nakatomi Plaza."

Jaxx snorts. "You can *Die Hard* another day, John McClane. Tonight we take the win. What's our out?"

Hawk points back the way we came. Down the hall, there's a bookshelf that sits waist-high. Hawk releases something along the side and it swings away from the wall. "The dumbwaiter. It's a series of tube slides that start on the top floor and ends in P1."

"Neato, adult shoots and ladders," Jaxx says, flashing a saucy smile. "Is Brant fittin' in these tubes?"

Hawk frowns but nods. "Almost definitely."

Brant snorts. "*Almost* definitely, that's awesome. So I guess I'm going last in case I clog the shoot?"

"Jaxx, you first," Hawk says, handing him one of his guns. "Secure the bottom. We're right behind you."

Jaxx grips the hand bar along the top of the opening and kicks his feet into the tube. "Yeehaw."

When he's gone, Hawk points to me. "Kotah, you're next." I

give Calli and Brant a quick kiss, grip the handle, and kick my feet into the slide. "P1, here we come."

~

Calli

The pain in Hawk's eyes as Kotah drops into the dumbwaiter without acknowledging him is heartwrenching. It cleaves me soul-deep to see them hurting one another when it's so obvious they love each other.

"You're up, Spitfire." Hawk shakes off the snub and gets back to the current crisis. "Be safe."

I reach to grip the handle and the world explodes.

Another wave of Black Knight fighters puke onto the top floor with us and start firing. Brant grabs me and throws me down the hall like I weigh no more than a duffle bag. I'm out of the way as the explosion takes out the wall where I was standing a moment ago.

The good thing about Brant's size is that when he puts his mind to it, he's big enough to screen the people he cares about from the oncoming danger. The bad part of that is that when he puts his mind to it, he acts as a screen between the people he cares about and the oncoming danger.

Bullets fly as Hawk grabs my arm and pulls me to my feet to drag me into his office. Brant's footing is sloppy as he staggers in behind us.

"Get off me and help Brant." I pull free of Hawk's grasp and flame up to a woman on fire. Standing on my own, I find my footing and stand tall, challenging the fuckers who dare attack my men.

With the heat and violence of hell's fury burning inside me, I throw out my hand and a stream of flame shoots from my palm. *That's new. Cool.*

The first line of attackers bursts into a screaming bonfire and I laugh. "Serves you right, ash-holes."

Hawk pushes his door closed and locks us in. Slapping his hand on a security scanner behind the door, he waits for it to activate and then taps something in.

Metal locks into place with a clank and then Hawk's all about us again. "That won't hold them for long."

"Tell me you have another safety straw of escape in here," I say, searching for a way out.

"Sorry."

"What about the roof? Can we get to the helipad? Maybe they left us their chopper."

He shakes that off too. "Not from here. Roof access is at the other end of the hall."

The rhythmic *boom, boom, boom* against the door indicates that our well-armed friends have no intention of giving up. "How much firepower do we have left?"

Brant coughs a laugh. "We've got endless leather whips and crops in the secret sex room."

Hawk frowns. "We're outgunned."

I file away Brant's comment about secret sex rooms for later and search for an answer. I'm getting better at calling my phoenix but if history has taught me anything, it's that I'm inconsistent and lose power at the most inopportune moments. I would hate to be our last defense and flame out in the clutch.

A loud crash brings me spinning around to see Brant going down. On an uncoordinated stagger and stumble, he takes out Hawk's coffee table and lands hard on the fancy area rug.

He has likely dented the concrete floor beneath.

"Double shit." I rush to him. "How bad is it?"

Hawk pulls away Brant's shirt and it's hard to tell where all the bleeding is coming from. "Fuck, Bear. Could you be a bigger target?"

He coughs. "Well, Papa Bear always said, if you're gonna do something. Do it big."

The rhythmic thumping against the door is gaining strength.

"I need to cry for you." Adrenaline is pumping in my veins and I don't know if I can calm down enough under pressure to call on my more tender emotions, but I have to try.

He shakes his head. "You're too keyed up. There's no time. You two need to get out of here."

"Like fuck," Hawk snaps.

I point my thumb at our eloquent Alpha. "Yeah, what he said. We're not leaving you. And besides, we already went over that. There's no way down."

"For me," Brant says. "You two are both birds. Bust the window and fly out of here, beautiful. You have to."

He coughs again and my mind stalls out. "No way. There's no way I'm leaving you here. Besides. I don't fly. I crash and burn."

"One time," he says, chuckling. "You're stronger now."

"Once was bad enough. That was over vacant farmland. I can't take out half of New York City. I don't want to go down in history with Mrs. O'Leary's cow taking out Chicago."

Hawk frowns. "Unfortunately, I don't think we've got much of a choice, Spitfire. You need to live. If we die here it's more than three deaths... there are two realms of fae depending on us. You've got this."

Laughter bubbles up my throat. "I don't 'got this'. You haven't taught me to land yet."

"Manhattan is an island, Calli. Aim for the Hudson and splash land." As if the discussion is over, he grabs his fancy, brushed metal lamp and swings it like a very long bat. The weighted base smashes through the glass wall and gives us our exit.

The *crash* is deafening and shattered shards rain onto the

ebony hardwood. Wind rushes in and whips my hair into my face, whistling through the room at a wild velocity.

Hawk tosses the lamp and grimaces at me. "We're flying out of here, Spitfire. You have to do it. It's the only way we all survive."

"All? How?"

Brant shakes his head. "Forget it, I'm too fucking heavy for her, and I can't swim. I'd rather die here with a gun in my hand holding them off for you guys to get away."

"Fuck that. I'll fly right beside you two. If you sink, I'll get you to shore."

My brain's slow to catch up but... "You think I can carry Brant?"

"Of course you can." Hawk hooks under Brant's arms and drags him toward the rush of wind invading the office. "You're a fucking mythical beast firebird. You trump all of us, hands down. You just haven't realized it."

The door creaks under the strain of bombardment and I jump. "I can't. I'm not."

He kicks away glass and lays Brant in front of the opening. Then, he grabs me by the arms and shakes. My teeth rattle as he pushes up in my grille. "You are the fucking fae phoenix. Those men will come in here and kill us in one minute. They poisoned Kotah. They shot Brant full of holes. We all die if you let them win. Where the fuck is John McClane? You were right. This *is* Die Hard, not the Alamo."

Brant coughs and I take in his current state of swiss cheese. I let all the fear and rage I feel inside me escape.

The terror of seeing Kotah on the ground.

Of Brant dying here because I fail him.

Of letting Hawk's father destroy everything he spent his adult life building.

I even feel bad for Jayne's father being made a pawn in their game.

Pushing my arms out to the side, I flame up and then go further. I call my phoenix forward and let the beast inside me loose. I practiced this at Brant's ranch and have a better feel of things now. Brant's right. I *am* stronger now.

My body explodes in size and ferocity.

I duck my head when it hits the ceiling.

"They are here to kill us, Spitfire," Hawk says, pulling out his phone and texting. "Protect your mates. Grab Brant and fly him out of here. I'm right here with you. You can do this."

The door gives way and I turn. The world feels strange from this viewpoint but I look down at the tiny men and shriek. Breathing a fiery wall of flames at them, I push them back into the hall.

Carefully, I clasp one of my talons around Brant's body and push off the edge of the building. One thing I learned over the past two days with Kotah is that it's okay for the wildling animal to ascend and take control.

My animal side is more confident and possesses stronger natural instincts. I let her take charge and give her wings.

Just please, don't let me kill Brant.

CHAPTER ELEVEN

Kotah

J axx and I descend to the ground as planned and wait at the bottom of the dumbwaiter chute for our mates. They don't come. Nerves turn into worry and worry twists into the realization that something went wrong. The others aren't right behind us as they should've been. "We need to go back."

"With the elevators locked, it'll take too long to get up to the thirtieth floor again."

"What do we do?"

Jaxx curses. "I don't know. I don't know how to help them."

The buzz of a text has us both outing our phones. It's a status update from Hawk. *Trapped and going airborne. Brant's hit. Head to the Hudson.*

"Oh, shit," Jaxx says, his thumbs flying over his screen. "Okay, Lukas is grabbin' the truck and comin' for us."

The scream of rubber on concrete brings a black SUV barreling through the parking garage at us. The two of us pile in and Lukas hits the gas. "Where am I going?"

Jaxx grabs his seatbelt and buckles in. "Hawk says head to the Hudson."

Lukas frowns. "That's really fucking helpful."

"Sorry. That's all we got."

The street looks like a warzone: the FCO staff has pooled out onto the concrete frontage, the police cars pulling up with their lights flashing, the cars slowing and honking, trying to figure out what's going on.

"Do y'all see anythin'?" Jaxx leans against the dash and is searching the skies as we drive.

I open the moon roof and stand on the middle bench. "Not yet. A mythical phoenix flaming her way across the Manhattan skyline will cause one major exposure incident."

"We'll burn that bridge when we come to it."

"There." I point but, of course, they can't see that. "Two o'clock. She's heading back towards New Jersey."

Thankfully, Lukas knows how to drive these streets because Jaxx and I would be tied up in traffic and no use to them as backup. "Keep an eye on them, Wolf."

Like I could look anywhere else.

Jaxx joins me in the open roof and I point to the orange streak in the sky. "*Damn*, she's a sight."

"She is."

"Do you see Barron?" Lukas shouts inside the truck.

"No, but it's hard to see anything around her. She's giving off a lot of light."

"I see Brant, though," Jaxx says, pointing. "She's got him in her talon."

My jaw drops. "He's got to weigh a ton."

"She's spectacular, Lukas. Not only is she flyin', but she's also airliftin' our bear to safety." Jaxx and I are still smiling up in awe when he looks at me and frowns. "Wait. Why are we headin' for the Hudson?"

I grab my hair and pull it back out of my face. "What do you mean? Why the worried face?"

"Because Brant can't swim. He told me that the first week when Calli got rocket-launchered into the farmer's pond. A bear's muscle density makes him sink like a solid boulder in the water."

I scratch my head and track their descent in the sky. "Do you think he mentioned that to them?"

Jaxx shrugs. "Was he conscious? Do they have a plan? Will Calli flame out completely when she hits the water? Does Hawk think he can rescue them both?"

Damn. It's hard to believe being separated for ten minutes turned into such a shit show.

~

Hawk

She's doing it. I didn't think she had the strength or control over her phoenix to get Brant out of there, but once again, she proves I should never underestimate her. With Brant clutched in her left talon, she pumps those amazing wings of fire and sends warm thermals swirling over me. It's official—I am so fucking head-over-heels in love with her it's ridiculous.

When we clear the Hudson, I wonder what she's doing. Why is she improvising? I told her to land in the Hudson.

Does she know where and what the Hudson is?

Oh, crap. Now what?

I don't know what to do to help her or figure out how to talk her down. She's right. I haven't taught her how to land. I should have made that a priority. With everything else that's been happening, I lost sight of so many things. Jayne. My father. Hunter. The crimes against the fae. The treachery within my company.

Maybe I'm not such a hotshot corporate mogul after all.

Or maybe I can't be when I have other, more important things occupying my mind.

And occupying my heart.

I can't believe how mating these four has changed my perspective on life. I wasn't lying when I told Jayne I'm happiest when I'm playing drinking games and hanging out with my mates. I never thought I'd be *that* guy, but it's true.

Calli, Jaxx, Brant, and Kotah are my everything.

Kotah. My heart clenches. How can he think he's not enough? He is everything... and more.

I know all too well how having a cold and disapproving father can make you feel like you're worth less than other people. I lived through that. Kotah did too. It guts me that he thinks that's how I see him.

I scan the forested grounds up ahead and it dawns on me where we are. She's back in Montclair. She flew Brant home instead of crashing him into the river.

But where will she land?

How will she land?

Calli

Giant fiery crapballs... And I was doing so well too.

I'm strong in the air today, the wind a cool comfort in my face. I feel the power of my phoenix bursting in my cells and feeding my wild side. With everything going so well, I didn't want to drop Brant into the river with those barges and boats. That water was murky and I hated the idea of it getting into his wounds.

I planned to take him back and drop him into the pool behind Mama and John's house next door. Clean water. No gawky people in every direction. Doc close at hand. And a quick rescue to pull him to the pool deck and cry over him.

Jaxx's parents might get a few shocking moments out of it. Starting with three of their son's mates dropping in from the sky and ending with me naked and bent over Brant, but like everyone keeps telling me.

Naked doesn't mean the same thing to wildlings.

I knew the general direction of the Montclair properties and once I spot the large patch of green that makes up the nature reserve, I find the one street that protrudes into the treeline. The three houses on the end of the cul de sac are the goal. Now, I figure if I fly low and drop him, I can circle and try to land.

I wish Hawk and I took the time to work on this.

I stop pumping my wings and get a sense of how quickly I sink toward the ground. I'm more like a glider than a stone, which is good. My first experience was the opposite. A shout from below brings my attention to Doc and Keyla training in the back lawn of their house.

I try not to get distracted.

Crashing and culverting a field is one thing. Taking out my sister-in-law and smushing my husband into the ground at the same time is quite another.

The good news is, Doc's there and he'll get Brant. Maybe? I know they can't swim but can they do nine feet of water? Gawd... we need to learn more about one another.

With a tilt of my wings, I swoop lower and focus on the twenty-eight-foot rectangle. I come in from the long end like a plane on a runway and drop him as gently as I can as close as I can. The splash is enormous and it scares me that it'll be too much for him. I push my wings back, causing resistance to forward motion, and turn to see that he's all right.

The last thing I see is John and Mama running across their lawn and diving into the pool.

Hawk shrieks beside me and I turn to face where I'm going

just as my talon catches on the roof of our shed. The sudden contact tips me forward and I faceplant into the dirt, flipping face over tail-feathers as my wings slap helplessly on the ground and the world spins in a violent series of somersaults.

When I stop, I close my eyes and groan.

Thanking my phoenix for all her help, I release my wildling side and flame out.

"Fuck, Calli." Hawk grabs a chunk of turf off my face and pitches it. "Are you okay? That landing was brutal."

"Seriously, that was an improvement."

He bursts out laughing. "You're shitting me, right?"

I wince as my bones knit back together and my lungs refill with oxygen. "Not even a little bit. I'm way less broken than usual."

"Okay, then shit yeah, we need to work on your landings." When I raise my hand, he clasps my wrist and helps me sit. "Because that was bad. Watching where you're going will be our first lesson."

"Help me get to Brant."

Hawk pulls me to my feet and wraps an arm around my hip. "How are you, really?"

"Shaky, but hey, we're not dead."

"I hate that that's our high bar."

Keyla races over looking frantic. "Where's Kotah?"

"They got out of the building," Hawk says. "Text them and tell them we're here."

"Where's Brant?" I ask, searching the back yards.

"John and Doc took him onto your deck for some privacy. Doc says you'll have to heal him."

I figured that. "Thanks."

Hawk keeps us moving. He helps me up the deck steps and over to the grapevine and latticed area by the hot tub.

"Are you guys all right?" Doc asks.

I nod. "Jaxx got shot in the shoulder but he didn't slow

down, so I don't think it's bad. You might want to be ready for him though."

He nods and places a solid hand on Brant. "I leave you in good hands, buddy. I'll check on you in a few."

To my relief, Brant isn't as dead as I feared. He's still shot and bleeding, but his eyes are open and he's breathing.

It doesn't take much to make me cry.

I'm tired and weary. I look at him, hurt and bleeding, and imagine not being able to help him. I think about Kotah's brush with death because someone poisoned him. I think about the look in Hawk's face when our wolf kissed me and Brant goodbye but not him. So many things have hurt my heart the past few days the tears come freely.

As they do, Brant pulls me onto his chest and holds me tight. Connected from head to toe, him bloody and gross and wet and me naked and still hot to the touch, we lay there while I find my center again.

We all made it out.

After a long while, his hand runs a slow circuit from my shoulder to my ass and then back again. My ear is pressed to his chest and I listen to his pulse and breathing as they get stronger.

Thank goodness.

"I am so blessed to have the magical miracle cure."

He chuckles beneath me and pushes up with his hips. "I have a magical cure for what ails me too. It's long and hard and needs a little help in gaining freedom."

I lift my head and blink at him. "Seriously? Right here? You were half dead ten minutes ago."

"Never know, I still might be. You better take my temperature. Help me get my thermometer out."

Hawk kneels and unbuckles his belt. "And you said I sexed you enough for a lifetime."

Brant flashes him one helluva hot look and lifts his hips off the wood of the deck. "Oh, I stand by that. I'd just like some of

Calli's other magical fluids. You know... to ensure a full recovery."

"To be thorough, you mean."

Brant nods. "Exactly."

I'm about to suggest we move this inside when Brant shifts his thigh to open my legs and pushes me down his body. His cock pushes inside an inch or two and my breath leaves me in a rush.

He gives me a moment, playing at my entrance before he impales me fully.

"I can't help it, beautiful. Every time the world threatens to take you from me, my wildling side gets possessive."

"And horny," I add.

His chuckle bounces me on his chest. "Yeah, that too."

Giving in to the mating madness, I drop my face and absorb the glory of his size stretching me wide. "Hawk, you better warn the neighbors not to swing by to check on the patient. Doc said he was coming back."

"Consider it done."

Jaxx

By the time Lukas pulls into the driveway, my jaguar is snarling and raging wild. Hawk had no idea they would be ambushed after Kotah and I took the tube ride but it doesn't matter. My mates faced danger and death without us. From what Keyla told Kotah, Brant was in rough shape when my parents pulled him from the pool.

"Jaxx." My father pulls the door of the truck open the moment the wheels are stopped. "Are you all right, son?"

"Fine, Daddy." I jump out and kiss Mama's cheek when she moves in to check beneath the sling Kotah rigged up for me.

"It'll be fine. Forgive me. I need to get to them. I love you both."

"We love you, too, baby boy," Mama says. "Go. Be with your mates. I believe they're out back on the deck."

She doesn't have to tell me twice. Kotah's already through the door and heading through the house. The mating scent coming off his skin is strong and I know from personal experience what the kid is going through.

Fearing for the life of your mate stirs up a carnal need that must be sated at the earliest opportunity. The idea sets my jaguar on another tack completely.

I follow Kotah because his nose has never steered us wrong. And yep, Mama's right. They are, indeed, on the back deck. Calli's riding Brant slow and deep and it looks like the only death Brant is approaching is the 'little death' of orgasm.

Nice.

Hawk sees us and launches out of the lounge chair where he's sitting to enjoy the show. As quickly as he moves toward us, Kotah diverts to get around him. It doesn't fly. Hawk blocks our passage. "Are you two alright?"

"Fine." I step in close and palm his cheek. Bringing our lips together, I show him how relieved I am that he's not dead. When I ease back, both of us are a little breathless. "Glad to see everyone is well here too. I think I'll join the fun."

He nods. "I wanted to wait for you two. Kotah and I need to iron out a few things."

"No. We don't." Kotah tries to push past us and Hawk grabs his wrist and locks a hold on him.

"Enough, Wolf. I've been in the dog house for two days and I get to have a say. You ripped me one and dropped to the ground before I got my chance to speak."

"Actions speak louder than words." He says, pulling at his wrist. "I've had a rough two days too. Maybe you should steer clear of me for a bit."

I suddenly want to be anywhere but in the middle of this. "Y'all need a moment. I'll go spend some time with Calli and Brant. Take the house for as long as y'all need it."

"We don't need the house," Kotah snaps.

"The hell we don't." Hawk gives me another quick kiss and a private smile. "Enjoy. And yes, we need some privacy to have this out. Thanks."

I take that as my cue and get outta dodge. Whatever is going wrong between Hawk and Kotah is about to come to blows and I, for one would rather be a lover than a fighter.

CHAPTER TWELVE

Kotah

Jaxx closes the glass door leading to the back deck and my wolf snarls inside me. My adrenaline spikes and my control on my wolf slips. I don't want to be here. I feel trapped.

"Kotah, what the hell?"

I shake my head to focus and smell Hawk's blood. He's clutching his arm above his wrist, scarlet liquid seeping up between his fingers. I glance down to my hand and am surprised to see my claws extended.

"You need to give me space, Hawk. I'm not in control of my wolf right now and you trapping me isn't helping."

"Then let's fix this. Give me the chance to make things right with you. We need to smooth this out."

My wolf is raging inside me and I want to flip forms but I can't trust what my wilder side might do. "Forget it. Just let me go, Hawk. There's nothing to smooth out. I'm fine."

"No. You're not. You think you've got things all figured out but you're so off base it's killing us both." He rips a strip off the curtain and wraps his arm. "I don't care if I end up with my throat torn out. You *will* hear me out."

I lower my head and narrow my gaze. "Don't tempt me."

"Don't make me push my alpha status on you. I want us to come at this on a level playing field."

I chuff. "That's a joke. You're an autocratic bully that always gets what he wants. You love pushing your alpha."

"Okay, let's start there. If I'm such a fucking bully, do you think I'll give up before I have my say? No. Good. That's the first thing you've gotten right in days. If you're stirring for a fight, we can—"

My left hook connects with his cheek and his head snaps back. Blood sprays the air and the scent makes my wolf even wilder. Hawk staggers back and hits the back edge of the sofa.

The only good part is that he's out of my way.

I take my freedom to move out into the hall and up the stairs two at a time. My emotions are high and I won't allow him to coax me into doing something the others won't forgive. Mating three out of four isn't horrible.

I can live with that.

"Kotah, stop." Hawk bolts up the stairs after me, cursing all the way. "Hit me if it makes your wolf feel better, but it doesn't change anything on my side."

"Big surprise. Nothing I do ever changes things on your side. Message received loud and clear."

I head into the master bedroom. I'm covered in blood and smell like gun powder from the battle at Hawk's office. My senses are overloading and it's not helping my control.

My clothes hit the floor with a flop and I head into the bathroom. If he won't leave me alone, I'll do my thing until he gets the picture. It works. By the time I finish taking a piss, I'm alone in the bathroom. I turn on the shower and step under the heat of the spray to wash my day off.

The spray feels good but I'm overly exposed being naked

when Hawk and I are both so keyed up. I make it quick. Once the smell of death is off my skin, I slick my hair back and step onto the puffy floor mat.

The air-conditioning against my heated skin is uncomfortable, but the least of my concerns. I wring out my hair and wrap the towel around my hips. When I get back into the master, I frown.

"Why are you still here?"

He drops to one knee and holds a black velvet box. "You said actions speak louder than words. So, how's this for you? I ordered these a month ago and had them engraved last week. I was planning a big romantic group ask, but fuck that now."

"And this is supposed to mean something to me?"

"It could if you let me in."

I look at the closed door and gauge my chances of getting over there and out before he tries to stop me. "I tried to let you in. I left that door so wide open for so long it nearly killed me. No more. I know who I am and I'm not them. I get it."

"No, Kotah, you *don't* get it." His voice booms and rattles the windows. "I love you."

I stare at him, numb. "I get this is you doing your corporate push to try to close a deal but that's low. You don't get to say those words to me. My heart is off the table. The offer is rescinded."

"That's your animal talking. We both know he doesn't like me much at the moment."

"And who's fault is that?"

"Mine—no question—I'm not denying that. Look," Hawk gets up from kneeling before me and clenches the ring box tight in his fist. "I know you think me telling you I love you is lip service, but it's not. I fucking love you."

"Those are just words."

"No, they aren't," he snaps, his eyes glassy and threatening to brim. "I haven't spoken those words to anyone since the day my mother died. I wasn't ready. I'm telling you now because you need to hear it and I need to get over myself and say it."

Seeing tears pooling in those steel-grey eyes tweaks my empathy and I sigh. Fuck me. My skin erupts into a wash of goosebumps. "And you haven't said it to them?"

He takes a step closer and offers his empty hand. "Feel the truth of what I'm saying. Please, don't shut me out."

"Like you shut me out?"

He swipes at his cheek with his curtain-wrapped wrist and leaves a smear of blood on his cheek. "Never again," he whispers. "I swear, I'll make it right between us but you have to give me room to fuck up... because I will."

I have no doubt he will.

Against my wolf's instincts, I accept his proffered hand and tap into the maelstrom of his emotions. Yeah, he's a mess. But he's genuinely aching for me to love him back.

"The reason I hesitated mating you isn't because you're not enough. It's because you're far more than I deserve. I'm cynical and twisted and you're perfect. I knew I would ruin things with you and that's exactly what I did."

I open my mouth to argue but he shakes his head. "Let me finish. Please, Wolf. Let me get this out."

I hate to feel the panic and uncertainty swirling inside him. I edge back to the end of the bed and look down to adjust the towel instead of looking at him.

I can't meet his gaze.

There's just too much of me at stake here.

"Kotah, I want you to be my mate. Not simply one of four because you were chosen, but mine. One-on-one. It's not because of the mating bond or even because you're fucking delicious in a towel. I want you to be my mate because I love you and would be honored to share my life with you."

I pick a piece of lint off my thigh and shake my head. "Then why am I last to be picked? If you love me so damned much, why do I feel like the shit on the bottom of your shoe?"

I wait for his big explanation.

When nothing comes, I—Oh, shit.

He's staring at me, tears staining his cheeks. "Is that really how I make you feel? You think you're shit on my shoe?"

I want to take it back, but... "At times, yes."

"Fuck me." He releases my hand and steps off, giving me his back. With a rough hand, he wipes over his face and pulls a deep breath. "You see, *this* is why I was so afraid to love you. I'm toxic. I knew I'd ruin the pure joy inside you and it's already happening."

The omega in me can't stand to see his grief, especially knowing I caused it. My nature is meant to calm others not torment them. "I'm sorry. I shouldn't have said that."

He waves that away and shakes his head. "Of course you should. I needed to hear it. For a minute, I almost had myself convinced it would be alright. I was right the first time. You need to steer clear of me."

"No, wait. Don't take it back." I reach forward and try to send him a rush of calm.

He throws his arms up and backs away like me touching him would burn him. "You're so much better not getting sucked into my bullshit. This whole mess. The attempts on your life... it's my father's poison. I thought I was clear of it, but I'm not. I'll taint you as he tainted me."

When he straightens and heads to the door, it's me who moves fast to block him this time. "No way do you say you love me and then walk out this door. Fuck your father. Fuck protecting me from who you are. You asked to mate me, now give me my fucking ring and mate me."

~

Hawk

I pull the ring box out of Kotah's reach and lock my elbow to keep him at a distance. "Didn't we just confirm that I'm terrible for you?"

"No. We confirmed that we love each other enough to be shitty to one another and hurt each other deeply. The lesson here isn't to quit loving each other, it's to be more careful."

"Kotah," I say, backing away. "I'm serious. I don't think you understand who I am. I destroy people for a living."

"You can, but you don't always. You have another side to you too. A side that I admire and respect." He reaches to where his towel is knotted at his hip.

I curse and lunge forward gripping the tuck of his towel before he can do what I know he's about to do. "I'm a bad idea. You need to listen to your wolf. Keep your guard up and keep your distance."

"Too late." He grips my shredded arm and when I scream, he pries the ring box from my fingers.

I struggle with him and somewhere in the scramble of arms and grabby hands, his towel ends up on the floor. Shit. That's not going to help my resolve.

I step back. "Kotah, give me the ring back."

"No." He rushes to the door and plants his back against the wooden panels. He has the box open in the next moment and slides the platinum band onto his finger. When it settles against the knuckle of his ring finger he flashes me a triumphant smile. "My answer is yes."

"No. There's no question."

"You're right. No question at all. Glad we agree." While holding up his left hand, admiring his ring, he drops his right hand for a casual stroke down his six-pack. "Now to seal the deal. Where do you want me?"

I roll my eyes and check the windows. Aside from pulling another swinging lamp line drive, there's no getting out of here except through the wolf and the door at his back.

The little shit tugs his cock and lets off a groan. "If only I had a tall, dark, male to help me with this." He turns his back to me, presses his left hand flat on the panel of the door, and keeps his right hand in front, working his erection. "Here I am, alpha. I dare you to claim what you know is yours. No. I double dare you."

He groans again and I swallow, fighting my nature to ignore the taunt. Everyone knows not to dare an alpha. Yeah, he's wily and too smart for his own good.

I take in the ass he's offering up and curse.

My mouth is watering and my cock is trapped behind the fly of my ruined Tom Ford slacks. With his palm braced against the door, he shifts his feet and widens his stance.

Fuck, he has a perfect ass.

The kid is smooth, tanned skin over carved muscle over a strong, young frame. His ass cheeks dimple as he shifts his weight and there's nothing I want more than to follow the muscled vee that leads from his hips to his groin.

He flips back around and I get a full-frontal view. His tip is glistening and swollen and his hand is gripped tight enough that when his stroke reaches his crown, cum oozes free.

"Yes," he says, his voice laced with a growl. "Yes to whatever you're thinking. Yes to your mouth. Yes to your cock. Yes to trussing me up and fucking me blind. Whatever you want from me, my answer is yes."

As he spouts off the possibilities, erotic images flash into my mind. I want every one of them but...

"What if this is a mistake?"

"Are you saying you don't love me?"

"No. I do." Standing there, staring at him in all his male glory, how could I not? He's the whole fucking package. "You are the ache in my chest, the fire burning in my balls, the tightness in my lungs. You're smart, refined, compassionate. You are the balm on my battered heart."

"Then come love me. I promise you won't ruin me. My wolf and I are strong enough to survive even you. And honestly, once you give in, I bet you won't find loving me nearly as intimidating. I'm just me, Hawk. Your wolf."

"Fuck. Why do you have to say perfect shit like that?"

He pushes off the door, striding forward, the predatory nature of his wolf in fine form. The whole time he's closing the distance between us, he tugs on that iron rod in his grip.

"Like what you see?" He stops a foot in front of me and takes my hand. "It's yours for the taking."

When he puts his cock into my hand, my eyes roll closed. I used to think I was a strong male who could withstand any temptation. With Kotah like this, naked and determined, I realize I'm not. I'm needy. I need him and want everything he says we can have.

"Tell me again that you love me now that you're holding the sacred wand of truth."

I chuckle. "I love you, Wolf."

"I love you too, Hawk. Now, let's get you naked and smooth things out. That's what you said right? You want to smooth things out with me?"

Kotah unfastens my pants and they slide down my thighs to the floor. I toe off my shoes but refuse to release his cock and go for my socks. Gripping the two sides of my dress shirt, Kotah rips them apart and buttons bounce around us like a shower of confetti.

His grin is too funny. "I've always wanted to do that. I thought I'd give you a first too."

I bark a laugh. "By shredding a four-hundred dollar tailored shirt?"

He bites his bottom lip. "Put it on my tab. I have a feeling I'll be ripping more clothes off you soon."

I chuckle. "Have we unleashed something wild and carefree in you, Wolf?"

"Definitely, yes."

I love the sound of that. Shrugging what's left of my shirt off my shoulders, I stand before him and let him have his look. My tattoos flow front and back, from my neck down to my waist and down each arm to my elbows. They are an extensive depiction of fae history and though he's seen them, he's never had the chance to study them as he's doing now.

I straighten and stand very still as he trails the pads of his fingers gently over my inked flesh. He stops at the ring through my nipple and smiles. "I think I'm obsessed with nipples. I can't wait to play with this little ring with my mouth."

"Everyone has their thing. I look forward to it." I point to the bed and send him up onto the comforter. After ridding myself of socks, I open the bedside table and see what they stocked up on in my absence last night.

Just the bare-bone basics.

Huh, I'll have to work on supplying our homes better.

Tossing a bottle of lube and some condoms beside the pillow, I stretch out beside Kotah on the soft coverlet.

Lying on my side, I run a gentle caress from his shoulder, along the smooth line of his ribcage and over the rise of his hip. His skin is soft and perfect. It honors me to be welcome to touch him like this.

"You're a beautifully made male," I whisper.

"I was thinking the same thing."

I drape my top leg over his thigh and pull him in close. His skin is warm against the chill of the air and I absorb the sensation. "Do you mind if I don't truss you up and fuck you like I do the others? For now, at least for a little while, can we make love like this, warm and connected?"

"Why?" His brow pinches and I know it's because he thinks I don't see him that way, but he's wrong.

"It would be too easy for me to dominate you. That's my fall back. It's like connecting but it's safe because it's what I know and I'm in control. With you... I don't want the shortcut. I want us like this. I want to look in your eyes and feel your heart under my palm. I want to connect with you four at a higher level and I think it'll help me open my heart if we work on it together."

I brush my thumb against the tension in his brow and he nods. "For now... but I want to know that side of you too. I won't be put on a pedestal. I've been up on one my whole life and I despise it. I won't be cherished like that."

"I promise, no pedestal, but you'll be cherished." Taking his face in my hands, I claim his lips.

He comes to me so willingly it scares me. He's too hopeful. Too eager. Too trusting. His kiss is hot and possessive. Our wolf may have been a virgin when this all started, but he's been in Sex-Ed Bootcamp ever since.

I smile as he pushes me onto my back and climbs onto my chest. Straddling my hips, he slides his tongue into my mouth and starts grinding his cock against mine. Trapped between our abs, the friction of skin-on-skin amps things up.

So much for taking it slow.

It seems my wolf has other plans.

It's fucking hot that he's so hungry for me. He's not the last pick. He's saving the best until last. Shit, that's not right either.

"Get out of your head, Hawk. We're mating here."

"Right. Sorry."

I reach up beside the pillow, grab the lube, and squeeze out enough to slick things up. Reaching between us, I slide my hand past our two cocks and get Kotah prepped.

"There's no rush," I say, as he grips my cock and rises onto his knees. "We've got all—or fuck, yeah—you can just impale yourself on my cock."

Kotah shudders as he forces his body to accept me in a rush. There's no easing into this. He sits fully against my groin and smiles. "I want you inside me. I want your cum marking me. I want people to know I'm yours and you are mine. Now, I can fuck you or you can fuck me, but this is happening."

I chuckle. "I did not think you'd be this bossy in bed."

He flashes me a wicked smile and grips my nipple ring between his fingers. "Less chatter. More orgasms."

Allllrighty then. Leaning back into the cushion of the pillow, I grip his hips and start a steady rhythm of rise and fall. It takes a bit for the lube to spread and muscles to relax but then, we get a solid glide and slide going.

"You're breathtaking," I gasp, my gaze locked on him riding me. The clench and release of his muscles as he works my cock, the way his eyes roll back when I hit something delicious inside him, the way his chestnut mane flows loose around his shoulders and down his arms and sides, swaying with the rhythm of our joining.

"I love you," I say, meaning it to the marrow of my bones. Funny. As tough as it was to say at first, now those three words seem to want to spill out of me.

Gripping the globes of his fine and dimpled ass, I buck him forward and flex my hips.

He falls forward onto his hands and claims my mouth. With aggression I admire, he breaks the seal of my lips with his tongue. I sense the challenge of his kiss and meet every marauding stroke of his tongue with my own.

Adding more pelvic thrust, I amp up and raise the stakes. He groans and chuckles into my mouth.

"I can see you becoming addictive, Wolf."

"Then my evil plan is working." He waggles his brows and flashes a victorious grin.

I pause inside him, my pulse pumping strong and steady. His scent is seared in my mind, but I can't get enough of him this way. Pulling free of his depths, I flip him onto his knees.

Gripping his hips from behind, I readjust my knees, realign, and give it with everything I've got. Yes. I've got much more power in my thrust like this.

Kotah barks a grunt as I push back inside.

I know from time with Jaxx that a fast reentry burns. It's a pleasureful pain for me. It strikes me too late to wonder if Kotah will enjoy it. He's on all fours panting and the spice of his pleasure in my nostrils is my answer.

He's so responsive.

I bet I could do anything to him—no *with* him.

The power and hunger that builds in me as I slam home are incredible. They zing through my cells as sensation tingles in my groin. At this rate, it won't take long for the mating bond to respond.

Then he'll be mine.

I close my eyes and hammer forward, my breath catching in my lungs. His shoulder muscles bulge and flex as he braces against my strength and takes me into his depths.

"You feel good, Wolf. If you need me to dial it back, you have to tell me."

Kotah glances back, his cheeks flushed. "No. Don't dial anything back. Please."

The apprehension I felt about claiming him dissolves and maybe I'm selfish, but I don't have the strength to disengage. It's too late for me to see anything beyond what I want.

Nakotah Northwood.

I want the warmth of him, the calm, the compassion. I want his body, his heart, and his beautiful soul.

With the next forward thrust of my hips, the mating energy ignites between us. I groan, the decadence of push and pull compounding as our mating bond takes hold. The power of the bonding magic courses between us, swirling from my system to his and back again.

We both cry out as the fire of our phoenix ignites inside us and we glow with the golden aura of our bonding.

It's done. Kotah and I are mated evermore.

The quint bonding is complete.

CHAPTER THIRTEEN

Calli

"Yay team!" I smile at Jaxx and Brant lying sated and sexed as the final mating bond locks into place upstairs. "We did it. We should celebrate."

Jaxx chuckles. "Celebrate that the five of us are insatiable sex fiends? Isn't that what we've been doing the past hour and a half?"

I run a possessive hand down Jaxx's glorious sixpack. "That was celebrating that we made it out of the FCO with all our mates intact. Now, I suggest we celebrate the completion of our mission to unite as a fully-bonded quint. Two different things."

"And here's somethin' to celebrate," Jaxx adds. "Has anyone noticed my shoulder?"

I look at it and shake my head. "What about it?"

He chuckles. "I was shot. The bullet grazed the muscle here and tore up my arm."

"How is it better?"

Jaxx's grin is wide and white. "I think more than your tears have magical healin' properties. I think you have healin' juices too."

"Then why have we been wasting time having her cry?" Brant asks.

"Right?" Jaxx says, chuckling. "Because, given the choice, I know which way I'd cure what ails me."

"I'll drink to that." Brant rolls onto his knees on the living room rug and walks naked over to the cluster of bottles on the kitchen counter.

We've got a mini liquor store over there.

"Mama washed the blender and the glasses," Jaxx says.

"Then, I guess, I'm good to dive right in and play naked bartender."

"Looking good from here," I say. "And I've got Jaxx's apron in my duffle if you want to wear it."

Brant grabs some juice and cans of sodas from the fridge and starts concocting. "The first renovation this house needs is a full bar."

I wave that off and roll onto my belly and watch Brant's ass while he's mixing drinks. "The first renovation this house needs is soundproofing. Either that or Jaxx's parents and Keyla and Doc need to move further down the block."

Jaxx nips the fleshy round of my butt and then kisses the sting. "You need to worry less about what the people around us witness. Trust us when we say, in the wildling world, sex is part of our lives. I can't tell you how many times Laney and I walked through the house while my parents were bumpin' boots. They're almost as bad as the five of us."

I cover my ears when the blender starts up. Not because of the motor of the mixer, but to block out Jaxx's comment. No use. No matter how much I don't want to picture Jaxx's parents... urgh, too late.

Jaxx rolls to sit, leaning his back against the couch when Brant brings our drinks back. "Thanks, man."

I accept mine and drink it down. "Thank you, Bear. I appreciate you boys compromising your manly drinking tastes for my benefit. This is yummy."

Brant chuckles and pours me a refill. "Males won't admit it in the presence of other card-carrying males, but we like fruity drinks too. Most beer tastes like ass for the first can or two. The deeper you dive in the better it gets. These drinks are tasty from the get-go."

Jaxx finishes his and holds his glass out for a top-up. "And the umbrellas and swizzle sticks are cute."

I laugh. "I can't believe a rugged jaguar alpha like you said swizzle sticks are cute. You're too funny."

When Jaxx has his refill, I hold up my glass. "Here's to our mating bond sex being complete. Yay team." I drink but the two of them are staring at me with matching looks of cocked brow amusement. "What? We've all had sex and accepted everyone. Why are you looking at me like that?"

Jaxx lifts his knee and rests his arm across it. The shift in position gives me a glorious view but I try not to look. If I do, he'll see me checking out his junk, and then he'll get hard and it'll begin us down the neverending road of us having sex.

Again.

"You're right when you say all the combinations of joinin' have been covered between us as individuals, kitten, but you're missin' one important combination."

"I am?"

Brant's deep bass chuckle does naughty things to my girlie bits. "You're missing the grand finale."

I scowl at them both. "And what is the grand finale?"

Jaxx lets off a sexy purr and flashes a grin. "All five of us together and servicin' you at once."

I don't know what they see in my expression, but both of them bust up laughing. Brant brushes the back of his finger against my cheek. "Look, puss. Our girl is blushing."

I swallow. "Nonsense. After all the things we've done and gone through why would having four men sharing me make me blush?"

Brant shrugs. "Fuck if I know. It sounds hot as hell to me. I can't wait."

"And when you say servicing me… you mean I'm the focus of all of you?"

Jaxx nods. "We each need to release inside you in one sex session. The chemical culmination of our cum mixin' with your feminine juices is how to complete the bondin' ritual… among other things."

"Okay, I guess if that's what gets things done, I can suffer through but the tone of your voice when you say 'among other things' makes me think I'm not going to like the next part. The five of us having sex completes the bonding ritual *buuuut?*"

"But nothing," Brant says. "The second part isn't a but, it's more of an *and*."

"Semantics. Okay, I'll rephrase. A fivesome is how we complete the bonding ritual *annnnd?*"

Jaxx makes a face and I know he's hesitant to spill the beans. "It's also how the phoenix conceives."

"Conceives? As in gets pregnant?"

"Possibly." He holds his finger up to emphasize the point. "Keep that in mind. It's only a maybe."

"Still, a maybe is worth worrying about." I run my fingers through my hair wishing I had a few more drinks in me before this convo. "Tell me all of it."

Jaxx places his hand on my foot and squeezes. "Remember when we first had sex at the Bastion and you asked me about birth control?"

I suck back my second drink and hold my glass out for another. "Yeah, you said I was covered. That wildling magic would take care of me."

Brant nods and pours me another. "And it does. The wildling

magic connected to the phoenix states that only when all four of us mate you in a single session will you conceive."

"So, who's the father?"

"We all are, kitten. That's the magic. All the strengths and qualities of the four of us will blend with your genes to create our child."

Okay, that's pretty cool. No one feeling any more or less of a dad than any of the others is a good thing. "But I'm not ready to be a mother. We're only finding one another. I grew up more on the streets than off. I don't know the first thing about raising a... what would it even be? A bear, wolf, jaguar, or hawk?"

"A phoenix," Brant says. "Your wildling genes are dominant over ours. Our child would be a baby phoenix."

Jaxx takes my glass and sets both of our drinks down. Pulling me into his lap, he snuggles me in. "Let's not panic. Just because you *could* conceive, doesn't mean you will. And if you do, you have the four of us standin' right there with you, and Mama and Daddy already told me no matter where we go or what we need if they can be any help, they will."

"Your parents are wonderful, Jaxx," I say, my eyes stinging, "but it's not their job to raise my baby."

"*Our* baby," Brant says, dropping to the floor to cup my cheek. "Just think, you and me and Kotah and Hawk know everything we wished could've been different in our upbringing and Jaxx has the opposite knowledge. He knows all about growing up in a loving family. Between the five of us, we can handle anything."

Jaxx chuckles. "We're currently takin' on corporate corruption and battlin' to unite two realms, changin' diapers and singin' our baby girl to sleep at night is nothin'. It'll be fine."

"And hey," Brant says. "With Hawk as a baby daddy, the kid's already a multi-millionaire."

I shrug. "I don't care about that."

"I know you don't, beautiful," Brant says, brushing his thumb under my eye. "My point is it'll be fine. We have enough love and devotion and money and support behind us that *if* it happens, the world won't crumble. Our baby bird will be the luckiest wildling on the planet."

I draw a fortifying breath and force a smile. "Okay, I'll try not to panic."

~

Hawk

With my mating bond with Kotah locking into place, the fire of our phoenix sizzles over my skin. As before, I feel my connection with her, Jaxx, and Brant through the bond that connects us. My mates. They are close.

The magic is still tingling in my cells when Kotah groans, drops his head, and I'm struck again by all that gorgeous hair. So, fucking sexy. "I'm going to come inside you and leave my mark. Then we're going to do it all over again all fucking afternoon."

"Perfect," he breathes. "I dare you."

Again with daring the Alpha. Cheeky bastard. I laugh and smack his ass for that. He stiffens and shutters. The wave of arousal that hits my senses is pure and heady. "Oh, like that, do you?"

"Yes."

I give him another five star on the fleshy round of his ass and he drops his head to the pillows. "I do."

"Next time. I want you sweet and sexy this time, remember?" My cock throbs in argument but I won't give sway to the male I am by nature. If sensations bombard I'll claim him roughly. That's not what I want for my first time with Kotah.

He's different than any other lover I've ever taken.

He has no edge. No guile.

He deserves more than a wild lay. He deserves more from me. "We'll play soon enough, I promise. For tonight, just let me love you until you can't move."

He chuckles and flashes a smile over his shoulder. "Well, when you put it that way, I suppose I can wait. Tell me again that you love me now that we're mated."

I look at the platinum band on his ring finger and fight off the building of pressure. My release is pushing in and as much as I want to mark Kotah, I don't want my first time inside him to end. "If I do, I'll lose it."

"Mmm, then definitely tell me."

Gathering his hair, I wrap it around my fist and tug to the side to turn his face. "Lay down for me."

He collapses forward onto his belly and I go along for the ride. Turning his face to the side so he can breathe, I press his hips straight into the mattress. With my one hand tightening around his hair, I slide my other hand under his front and palm his cock. "Take pleasure from me while I take pleasure from you. Then I'll tell you."

The growl that escapes his chest hits me right in the balls. As I pump into the sweet grip of his ass, the power of my thrusts has him humping my hand. He's so hard and feels so good, a new hunger fills my mind.

"Mmm, don't lose it yet. I want to suck on you."

"Gawd, now you tell me?"

I chuckle and dish him a bit of his own medicine. "I dare you to hold off, Wolf. You want to plunge your cock in my mouth right?"

His whole body tenses and his jaw clenching as he fights off his release.

The rough panting of his ragged breath mixed with the tight constriction on my cock is too much. Too fucking sexy. The last of my defenses dissolve and my body goes rigid in a series of racking spasms. The orgasm I pour into him is soul-shattering… and seems endless.

I release my grip on his cock and switch my hold. Sliding my hands up his sides, I grip both his shoulders from beneath and leverage my strength. Lost in the mindless pleasure of emptying into him, I thrust harder.

"Fuck… I love you, Wolf," I gasp, my voice hoarse. "You're mine. And I don't want you to ever forget it."

Kotah's breathy shout and mattress humping signal that he's making one helluva mess on the new bedding.

Oh well, when you're having the sex of your life, cleanup is the least of your worries.

I nip the back of his neck and growl. "Couldn't hold out, I take it."

"Too good," he moans, finishing his love affair with the coverlet.

I chuckle. "Then, I'll keep fucking you like this until you're hot and hard again. Then, I'll suck on you as I planned. Tell me when."

"Oh, it won't take long."

Knowing I haven't got long to play, I enjoy my last moments filling him. His ass is as good as it looks.

"When."

"You're ready and hard for me?"

"Hells yeah."

I flip him on his back and shift down the bed. Drawing my tongue up the length of his shaft, I groan. His cock is rock solid and slicked with his release. He tastes like sex and nature and I'm so thirsty for him it's ridiculous.

"Oh… fuck," he groans, as I suck him between my lips.

I play a bit, getting a feel for him and his likes, and then, I bring him onto his knees so he's fucking my mouth.

I grip his shaft with a firm hand and suck him off. "Fuck my mouth," I say around his cock. "Cream down my throat."

The growl of his wolf increases and a split-second later, Kotah grips the headboard with one hand, braces his other palm beside my head, and lets loose. Pumping like his hips are powered by pistons, he proceeds to do exactly as asked and fucks the everloving shit out of my mouth.

I take it all, my hawk shrieking at the perfection.

The kid's hips are unhinged. The thrust and retreat action is wild but wonderful. I grip the base of his erection harder so I don't lose track of it.

Kotah has my heart pounding and my balls crawling tight to my core, burning with the promise of another release.

On a hard thrust to the back of my throat, his hips lock and he lets off a throaty hiss. The first rush of cum releases and spurts into my mouth in warm, salty waves. I swallow and suck and milk him for everything he's got.

More, give me more.

I don't know if it's one orgasm that lasts for ages or he keeps fucking my mouth and coming until I've had my fill, but by the time he collapses on the mattress beside me, it's dark outside.

"Fuck you taste good, Wolf."

His eyes are closed and his smile content. I crawl up behind him, collect him in my arms, and kiss his neck. With our naked bodies aligned, I'm so wet and slick with cum, I slide right in.

"I won't last long. You rest and let me love you."

"You do you, Hawk... or me, I guess. You do me."

I chuckle and move my hips in slow rhythm with delicious penetration. I'm a man of my word. After the adrenaline and emotion of the past hours, I grind him from behind for only a few minutes before I mark him again and my body finally rests.

"I love you, Nakotah Northwood. And—in case you haven't guessed it yet—you are thoroughly marked."

"Thoroughly," Kotah says, yawning.

Still connected, I close my eyes wondering who marked who

more thoroughly. By the unfamiliar sense of peace soothing my soul… I give him the win.

CHAPTER FOURTEEN

Calli

"Welcome back to the land of the livin'," Jaxx says. He pauses the movie and gets up from the couch to greet Kotah and Hawk as they join us in the living room. "You two must be starvin'."

"Famished," Kotah says. "And more than a little dehydrated, I'm sure."

I chuckle. "I am intimately familiar with that sensation."

Jaxx heads to the kitchen to heat them some of the leftovers from dinner. "Sex with an alpha can do that to you."

Hawk arches a brow and sends him a private smile. "And what does sex with *two* alphas do to you?"

Oh, hot. I luuurve when the two of them start throwing around that look. Whatever it is the two of them get up to I'd bet it's worth the price of admission to watch.

Jaxx's cat lets off a purr and all of us straighten. "Okay, enough sexy talk, or we'll all end up naked again. We've got real-world stuff to discuss."

"Agreed," Hawk says. "I have one order of personal business and then we'll get to it."

Jaxx dons the oven mitts and goes back to readying two heaping plates of food for our weary and sex-weakened mates.

I swing my feet off the couch and onto the floor. "Okay, go. You've got our attention. What's up?"

Hawk strides over to where I'm sitting in the living room and drops to one knee on the rug. He pulls out a black velvet ring box and winks. "My original plan was to wine and dine you all and do this up with romance and panache. That went out the window and I jumped the gun earlier and asked Kotah. He has agreed to officially be not only my mate but my husband."

Kotah holds up his left hand and flashes a sexy titanium band. The happiness beaming from our wolf makes my heart sing. Good on Hawk for getting our boy sorted out and locked into the mating.

"Since you were raised human and the ideals from that community still influence you, I thought it would be nice to honor your customs as well as our own. So, Calliope Tannis," he says, locking gazes with me, "will you be our wife?"

Hawk. The man who thinks of everything.

"Yes, I will."

"Well, hot damn," Jaxx says, carrying two plates of dinner over to the table. "I give you full points on this, hotness. Seein' the smile on her face makes me wish I thought of this myself."

Hawk opens the ring box and smiles. "It's a plain titanium band to match ours. I had Lukas spell it so it'll survive your transitions into phoenix and I had it engraved."

I accept the ring and tilt the band toward the light. "*Our fire.* I love it. I love *you.*"

"I love you, too, Spitfire."

I freeze, my pulse picking up pace. Did he just say…?

Hawk closes the distance and makes a gentle sweep across

my lips with his mouth. "Close your mouth. You don't have to look so shocked. I told you I'd get there. I love you."

My eyes are stinging and I don't want to cause a huge emotional scene, so I blink and try to regroup. "Will you put it on me?"

Hawk takes the ring and slides it on my finger. "If you would rather a gemstone, I can do that. I just thought with the battles and fighting, this was more practical... and you've never seemed that fussy about jewelry... but if it's not what you want—"

"—It's perfect," I say, interrupting his tailspin. "I said I love it and I meant it. I don't care for flashy diamonds or gems. It matches all of yours. That makes my heart ache. It's perfect."

The relief in his smile makes his gift that much more perfect. Yes, he can afford anything, but his gifts always reflect a depth of consideration I appreciate.

"What does yours say, Wolf?" Jaxx asks as Kotah sits at the table and accepts one of the plates.

"Our soul."

Hawk kisses me on the cheek and moves to Brant. Without preamble, our bear puts out his left hand. Hawk slides his ring into place. "Yours says, Our strength."

Brant admires the band on his hand and flexes his fingers. "Accurate and spank."

"Glad you like it," he says, moving to Jaxx. He rounds the kitchen island and stops right before our jaguar. "Our passion."

Jaxx waits until the ring is on his finger and then grips Hawk by both sides of his neck and pulls him in for a sultry kiss. "You rock my cock, Bastian. I love you so hard."

"I love you too."

That's the second time I've heard Jaxx call Hawk Bastian. I'll have to ask him about that privately some time.

"And what does yours say, Hawk?" Brant asks.

"Nothing yet. I expressed how I see each of you. I'll let you decide what you think mine should say when we get back to the engravers at the Palace."

Kotah's wolf lets off a warning rumble. "And what if I don't want to go back there."

Hawk shrugs. "Then we don't go back there. Simple as that. I've put the Fae Council and the Prime into a time-out for the moment. If we want to shake up how things are done, you and I are the two most politically powerful members of the realm. We can change the landscape."

"Yeah, baby," Brant says, coming over to the kitchen table to sit with us while Hawk and Kotah eat. "And we're sleeping our way to the top."

Jaxx nods. "There ain't no such thing as an indecent proposal. Remember that you two. There are no HR issues here. We're willin' to sex our way to the top. Blowjobs. Bendin' over. Whatever you need."

Hawk rolls his eyes and starts in on his dinner. "Okay, tell me what's been going on over the past—shit—five hours of fucking."

Hawk

It's nine o'clock that night when Lukas gets back from my office and comes in to update us on the status of things in Manhattan. He looks tired and I make a mental note to give him a month off when this is over—maybe two. "Jayne and Victor are safe and tucked away in your penthouse as instructed. The office is locked down, police and fire have gone through and they'll want to speak to you first thing to take your statement."

"What about them?" I ask, pointing to my mates.

"With a little manipulation, I was able to keep them out of it. According to our story, you came back from an extended absence, you got a call from the lobby warning you that hostiles were on the way up, you cleared the building, and when they reached upstairs, you and I fought them off and escaped through the dumbwaiter chute."

"Close enough. I can sell it. And what's the damage?"

"The top floor is a warzone. Other than that, the building remains sound and structurally secure. Throw some money at it, and you'll be up and running in a month."

Brant chuckles. "Throwing money at things is his best event."

I roll my eyes but he's not wrong. "Alright, take a month. Maybe by then, we'll have things sorted out with the realms. Oh, and I want this property up to snuff too. I'm thinking of a small stone castle. Calli mentioned she likes them."

Calli frowns. "I do, but don't spread yourself too thin. Fix the FCO Headquarters so people can get back to work, but we don't need a new and improved mate house here if we're headed off to open the portal gate. You don't have to take on every task in every direction."

I smile. "It's what I do. But I hear your concern and I agree, we need to prioritize."

"We need to get the Portal Gate open."

Lukas stretches his neck from side to side. "I don't mean to be indelicate... but how close are you all to getting Calli to full power?"

Calli shakes her head. "Seriously? Did everyone know about the grand finale except me?"

I grip her hand where it lay on the table and squeeze. "It's a matter of wildling lore, Spitfire."

The blazing blush of her cheeks is too cute.

I refocus on Lukas and sober. "We're close. I realize we've run out of time. Sure as shit, my father and whoever he's corrupted on the Fae Council will be gunning for us and digging in at the site of the Portal Gate at the same time."

"I think we should dispatch a team to the site of the Portal Gate and secure it as a preventative measure."

I nod. "Absolutely. Do that. And what about media fallout from Calli blazing across the city?"

Lukas pulls out his phone and calls up a video. "They'll know about Calli, all right. Jayne and I got this wiped from human news and planted a story of a glider that caught fire and drifted over the city. Fiske altered the memories of the sightings city-wide, but there are fae species who won't be affected by his mind manipulations."

"Okay, so we operate under the assumption that the great Black Knight knows we're on to him, we've blocked whatever he was manipulating behind the scenes, and that Calli can not only call her firebird but can fly and breathe streams of fire."

"Looks that way."

"So from what side do you think they'll attack us?"

Lukas shakes his head. "Hard to tell. I'd say your best bet is for the five of you to drop off-grid and get Calli up to full strength as soon as possible."

"Wait," Calli says, her brow furrowed. "When you say off-grid what do you mean?"

"I mean not anywhere Barron owns or the five of you have frequented. You five need to disappear for a bit and ready for the battle ahead. Full-strength, four soul shards to complete your pendant, training complete... including being able to land without taking yourself or your mates out of the battle completely."

The look on Calli's face is too fucking cute. "He's not criticizing your skills, Spitfire. He's objectively assessing our short-comings so we can make a tactical decision on how to best approach the next phase of our plan."

She leans back in her chair and crosses her arms. "Hmph, I'd like to see him land. It's not as easy as you think. Did you see how big my feet are when I'm a phoenix? No wonder I tripped over the stupid shed. And it's a stupid spot for a shed anyway. Right in the middle of the yard where someone can trip on it."

I kiss her knuckles and stand. "All right. We'll leave tonight. Get us a vehicle, stock it, and sweep it for any kind of tracking. If we're leaving our backup in the dark, I don't want to find ourselves alone against a horde. Also, we'll need burner phones, and we'll have to live small and pay by cash so we'll need a float. For a week or two, what do you think we'll need... fifty thousand in fifties and hundreds?"

Calli chokes. "Wow, your idea of living small and mine are realms apart. Last year I made thirty-eight thousand for the entire year."

I chuckle. "I'm not suggesting we'll need that much, but it'll be good to have it if we do. I won't have my mates going hungry on the side of the road if we breakdown."

Calli rolls her eyes. "Then yeah, fifty large should be good. We do, after all, have to feed Brant."

Calli

"On the road again," Jaxx sings, giving his best Willie impression, which, I'll admit, is pretty damn good. He's got a guitar in his lap and is sitting on the couch in the lounge area of our beloved tour bus.

Hawk is driving. Brant and Kotah are putting away groceries. And I'm sitting at the front with Hawk taking it all in. "I thought we were supposed to be off-grid. Aren't the bad guys going to recognize that we're in our own vehicle. They already attacked us in this once before."

Hawk casts a sideways glance and smiles. "It was available on short notice, and Lukas had it painted and changed the plates since our last adventure. He also kept it off the FCO fleet list and locked in his garage."

"Is he paranoid or psychic? Did he know we'd be here again so soon?"

"Lukas is extremely good at his job and a remarkable tactician. If he says this vehicle is clean and off-grid, I don't doubt it for a second."

"And, I guess it doesn't hurt that he poofed a magic spell on it before we left."

Hawk smiles and takes the ramp onto the highway going west. "I'm sure he'd prefer if you described what he did as casting a ward of protection on us, not poofing a magic spell."

"Potato-Tomato. Same thing."

He laughs. "No. It's really not."

We drive along for a while and I watch the yellow road lines appear in the wash of our headlights and disappear as we mow them over. Casting a glance back at the guys, I smile at the country music singalong going on back there.

"So you and Kotah worked out all the tension?"

He draws a deep breath and exhales. "Yeah. It was touchy there for a bit, but we got there."

"I'm relieved. It was twisting me up to see the two of you hurting."

"No more. We sorted through it."

Good. I'm relieved to hear it. "Sooo, this grand finale."

He licks his lips and bites back a smile. "Yes? What about it?"

"Well, you missed the convo when Jaxx and Brant briefed me, so I thought we should recap. I'm a little overwhelmed at the idea that I could end up conceiving during the mating orgy that gets me my full powers."

He chuckles. "I love that you consider it a mating orgy. That makes my night."

"Glad my mortification amuses you."

He sobers. "Apologies. I for one am looking forward to the

grand finale, as you call it. And knowing the other males, I can guarantee I'm not alone in that."

"I'll give you that. Aside from me envisioning my hoohaw dripping wet with the cream from all four of you, the fivesome sounds sexy."

"So does your dripping pussy." Hawk adjusts in his seat and runs a hand down the front of his pants. "Fuck, now I'll have that image burning in my mind for the next four hours."

I roll my eyes. "But getting my full powers means I might be endangering a baby by going into the battle at the Portal Gate. Is there any cosmic birth-control I can take? Does Lukas have a magic spell for that? So we can have the mating orgy without the worry of a baby?"

"*If* you conceive, and that's a big if, there's no danger to the baby other than you getting killed. In which case, it doesn't matter if you're pregnant or not, because you'll be dead. And no, Lukas does not have a magic spell to counter the magical intention of the universe. He's good but he's not that good."

I sigh, staring out at the night.

"Why are you more afraid of the baby aspect than the death by violent rebels? Do you not want children?"

I shrug. "It's not that. I'm pro-family when it comes down to it... I just figured that would be something we'd address years down the road once all this Portal Gate craziness is over. I mean, we don't even know what state the fae realms will be in. It just seems fast."

"And is that your only objection?"

I search his expression but can't tell where his question is coming from. "What else would it be?"

He shrugs, turning the dial to start the windshield wipers. There's a light mist starting and it's dotting the windshield. "I want to make sure you're not having second thoughts about committing to us long term. Entanglements get stickier with kids in the mix."

I frown. "Well, you can stop wondering about that right now, Mr. Barron. You're mine. This quint is mine. And I'm not going anywhere willingly. I'm a little unnerved that the universe can decide willy-nilly when I pop out kids. That's it. That's all."

Hawk snorts. "It's not willy-nilly. It's one time when all four of us release inside you. For the next five or ten years, we can leave it at three inside you and one inside Jaxx, or Kotah or Brant or me. There are measures of control beyond willy-nilly. Besides, with all the side hustle going on with your males, how often do you expect we'll all be around and all on the same page?"

"Not that often, I guess." I think about that. With Hawk running his business and Kotah's duties as Fae Prime about to take hold, there haven't been that many opportunities for all five of us to get together even if we wanted to. And yeah, even if it is all five of us, that doesn't mean they all need to finish inside me.

"Feel better?"

I nod. "Yeah. I do."

CHAPTER FIFTEEN

Hawk

 wake to silence on the bus and the sweet succulence of someone sucking on my cock. Eyes closed, I stretch and curl my pelvis, arching deeper into that mouth. "Now this is how every male should wake up."

"That's what I thought," Calli says, around my erection. "They sent me in to wake you up and I saw your morning wood and thought this is much better than an alarm clock."

"Infinitely better." I shudder as she grips my sac and squeezes my balls. "Where is everyone?"

"They got your note and are inside shopping. Kids in a candy store by now, I expect."

I chuckle and reach down to stroke my fingers through her hair. "They took the list, though, yeah?"

"Mhmm." The vibration of her affirmation against the swollen tip of my cock is perfection.

"And are we supposed to join them?"

"Mhmm."

I groan, pushing into that vibration. "How many questions can I think of where you'll answer me that same way?"

She chuckles, the effect is not nearly as erotic.

"Give my sac another squeeze, would you?"

"Mhmm."

Yep. There it is. The zing and sting of my balls getting fondled bring my hand up to my nipple ring. While she's going to town, I grip the hoop on my chest and twist it. "So fucking good."

"Mhmm."

"Are you good to swallow? Because I'm close."

"Mhmmmm."

My fingers tighten in her hair and she's riding my shaft with a hunger that always humbles me. Calli loves sucking cock. I draw a deep breath and the scent of her arousal does me in. My breath escapes in a throaty burst and my abs clench. When I stiffen, the heat of my release is so gratifying.

Calli swallows and sucks, growling like a primal animal.

"Oh... fuck." After another racking spasm and a second rush of cream, I settle and fall limp against the mattress of the back bedroom. When I'm once again able to form full sentences, I chuckle and pull her up to kiss her. "Good morning."

"Good morning." She sets her palm against my chest. "I'm officially applying to be your alarm clock for work."

"You're hired."

She laughs and rolls off the bed. "You should've held out for a second interview. Geez, Barron. Do I have to explain everything to you? I thought you were a shrewd businessman."

I chuckle and get up. "You're right. I was too eager and rushed the deal. I should've held out."

Calli meets me chest-to-chest and wraps her arms around my back. "We'll practice until you get it. There's always tomorrow morning."

"Perfect. I can hardly wait."

She kisses me again and heads out to the bus proper. "Get dressed. If we don't get in there soon, you'll own the entire store."

I grab my clothes off the back of the chair where I tossed them early this morning when I parked for the night. After pulling my black khakis up my thighs, I pull my t-shirt on and tuck things in. That's true, my husbands know how to shop.

Kotah

It's one o'clock that afternoon when Jaxx pulls our tour bus into an interstate rest area north of Fort Wayne, Indiana. He drives us around back and stops in one of the long, extended spots near the treeline of a wooded grove.

I step off the bus, fill my lungs with the clean, fresh air, and smile. "Remember the first rest stop we visited?"

Calli rolls her eyes and blushes. "I felt so bad for you."

Jaxx shakes his head. "I missed this one."

Hawk steps off the bus carrying the bags of merchandise we bought this morning. "We were closing in on the property Calli wanted us to check out to find her drow gangbangers and I stopped at a rest stop to regroup. Calli and Kotah were making out hot and heavy in the backseat of my SUV."

I close my eyes. "The smell of Calli's arousal and burnt leather upholstery will forever be etched in my memory."

Brant laughs and points over at us. "Calli got off, dry-humping the wolf's lap. She was naked after burning off her clothes and nearly caught Hawk's truck seats on fire."

"But we needed to get back to business," Hawk says.

"All too soon." I laugh, hardening behind my fly just thinking about it. "I needed a few minutes alone in the restroom before I could continue."

Jaxx grins. "Oh, the early days. So, you weren't a *total* virgin when our fiery seductress got hold of you above the roadhouse. You had spent time with the palm sisters."

"A lot of time." I take the five paintball guns out and lay them on the picnic table. "I didn't leave my room much in the teen years when I was living in the palace. If my nose wasn't in my books, my hand was in my pants."

"Damn straight," Brant says, his chest bouncing. "One day I'll tell you about the time Maggie and her agri-tour caught me tossing off behind the straw bales."

"Oh, no," Calli says.

Brant chuckles. "Oh, yes. Needless to say, those were interesting Yelp reviews."

Hawk shakes his head and pops the tab of a cider. After taking a long haul, he points to the gear. "Okay, first teamwork training game, capture the flag. Kotah and Brant versus Calli and Jaxx. I'll play the wildcard and will be against all of you. Pick your colors."

Calli picks up the green ammo and hands it to me. "Green is the color of frogs."

I laugh. "Hey, I was the last pick. You guys already picked red for blood and black for death."

"Good one," Jaxx says, grabbing black. "I'm death."

"Yep, I'll be bloodshed." Brant grabs the red.

Hawk goes for bright blue without any bravado and that leaves Calli with orange. Her grin widens. "Orange for the lick of flames that are going to burn your fine asses."

Brant's bear growls with pleasure. "Let's do this."

Calli raises her hand. "First, show me what I'm doing. I've never held one of these before."

I raise my hand as well. "I'm with Calli. We didn't get a lot of paintball wargames at the palace."

Brant frowns. "That's too bad for you. I bet there are a few people you would've liked to take a free shot at."

"You're not kidding."

Jaxx sidles over to us and holds up his weapon. The guns are sleek black and chrome numbers with long, slender barrels that stick out front and a plastic bottle up top that holds paintballs, and a small bottle below the handgrip.

"The gas pressure bottle under here propels the paintballs when you pull the trigger. The tube up top holds forty paintballs. This is your safety. Click it off safe, point, and shoot."

He looks at Calli and then me. "Sounds easy enough."

Brant pulls his goggles over his head and hands us each a pair. "Safety first, my lovelies. Fun's fun until you get a paintball to the groin."

Calli snorts. "And how do goggles help with that?"

"They don't. Speaking from experience—watch your aim. My nuts are having flashbacks and crawling inside me just thinking about it."

Hawk grabs his weapon, locks his blue paintballs into place at the top of his gun, and pulls on his goggles. "Warm-up here and give me ten minutes to hide the flags."

He holds up two pairs of Calli's panties and raises them high when she jumps at him. "What the hell, Hawk?"

"Added incentive, Spitfire. Whoever captures the panties most often over the next couple of hours gets dibs on planning the mating orgy."

I laugh at the sudden surge of testosterone in the air.

Between Hawk, Jaxx, and Brant, I don't care what they have planned. The five of us together for the first time will be awesome regardless of where we are or what's been planned beyond making love to our female.

"Challenge accepted." Jaxx meets Brant with a fist bump.

"Okay, give me five to set things up."

Calli shakes her head. "I can't believe you're hiding my underwear in a rest stop forest."

Hawk laughs, turning toward the trees, waving Calli's undies in the air. "The needs of the many outweigh the complaints of the few, Spitfire."

~

Hawk

"That was better." I shrink back from Calli's hostile glare and hold up my hands. "It was."

Jaxx picks the chunks of dirt off her and Brant helps her to her feet. "He's not wrong, beautiful. Comparing that landing to the ones you made while we were staying in the bunker, I'd say those were definitely better."

"Are you hurt, kitten?"

"Only my pride," she says. "I thought I did everything you told me and I still ended up kissing worms."

"Lucky worms." I laugh. Okay, she does not find me charming tonight. "Tell me what you thought you did right and I'll see what you forgot."

She looks back at the tangerine skyline as if to jog her memory. "I picked a spot to focus on. I dropped low, extended my feet, and right before I touched the ground, I flapped my wings backward to create drag to slow my forward momentum."

"Did you lean back?"

When she screws up her face and sighs, I can't help but smile. "It's a common error, Spitfire. Don't get down on yourself. Tomorrow's the day."

She checks the orange glow of the firey sun descending below the horizon. "Do you think I can get one more try in before I'm lighting the sky up instead of blending in?"

I shake my head. "Not worth the risk. All it'll take is one lookie-loo with a phone posting a video of the weird flaming sky and my father and his men will track down the IP address and have us cornered without backup."

She sighs again and I can't help but pull her in and pick grass and twigs from her hair. "How about a nice hot shower and Jaxx can massage what aches."

She arches a brow and smiles. "I have a lot of different kinds of aches. It might take more than just Jaxx."

I chuckle and brush the smudge on her cheek. "Do you think these aches of yours might take all four of us to ease?"

"I think maybe, yeah."

I meet her gaze and watch her pupils while I ask her the next question. "And you're sure you're ready for the four of us, knowing the chance of baby-making."

"I'm sure we can handle it. Is it alright to say I hope it doesn't happen? I don't want to give up all the wild and sexy just yet. Is that wrong?"

"There's no wrong answer, kitten," Jaxx says, hugging her from the side and kissing her head. "We'd rather hear the truth any day of the week than have you say something you don't mean for our sakes."

"Hells yeah," Brant says.

Kotah trots through the trees and flips to man mid-stride. His clothes flash on a split second after giving me only the briefest glimpse of all that fit and sculpted nakedness. "I made three circles sweeping out further each time. There's nobody around for miles. We are well and truly alone in the wilds."

"Good. Thanks, Wolf," I gesture toward the tour bus and smile. "Calli's going to take a shower, then we'll have dinner, and see where the night leads us."

Kotah reaches up to gather his hair and tie it back with the leather band around his wrist. "Yeah? Are you good with that, *Chigua?* Even knowing everything?"

I give her credit, Calli's not one to take her knocks lying down. She straightens and lifts her chin. "Sex with my four favorite lovers I look forward to. The rest... we'll take as it comes."

Kotah looks to me and I give him a reassuring smile. "You and Calli are the two that just worked out. Why don't you help her into the shower, sweet prince?"

The kid's expression lights up. "It would be my greatest pleasure."

"Not just yours," Brant says. "This is Calli's night."

"And I'm supposed to massage her and rub her down," Jaxx says. "I don't think you were here for that part."

Calli shakes her head and heads toward the bus. "Honestly, making sure all four of you get equal time and attention is going to be a full-time job."

I laugh and let the others lead. "Who said you're responsible for keeping the four of us entertained? We can be self-sufficient, can't we men?"

The naughty grins that flash between all of us as we head into the bus are too revealing.

Calli's gaze bounces around between us and she shakes her head. "You four are just too hot."

Brant

While Calli and Kotah are in the shower, and Jaxx transforms the bedroom at the back of the bus into a massage parlor, I pop one of Mama's homemade lasagnas into the pre-heated oven and then go out to check on Hawk. He said he wanted to fortify our security and when I get outside, he's got his hands up and is casting. I sit on the bottom step of the bus entrance and watch, trying not to disturb him.

Five minutes later, he drops his hands and the energy in the air drops considerably.

"So, how is it you have casting powers? I've wondered about it for weeks."

"Ah… seeing me do something magical must have redlined your distrust dial."

"And then Lukas gave you a transfusion. That threw me too. Wildling blood and human mage blood are not compatible. He never should've been able to save your life. But here you are."

Hawk gestures for us to go inside and I lead the way. He seals the door behind us and casts a quick ward there too. By the time we walk the fifteen feet to the lounge area to flop on the couches, my curiosity is piqued. "We're mates now. I hope you know that you can trust me with whatever it is."

Hawk grabs us each a beer from the fridge and hands me one. "My mother was a human mage. My father is avian."

I crack the tab on my drink and take a few gulps. "Then how are you able to shift into a hawk? Only pureblood wildlings can shift."

Jaxx comes in and sits on the arm of the couch. "I've wondered about this too. You don't mind if I join, do you?"

Hawk shakes that off. "No, it's private but not a secret. My mother wasn't just any mage, she was the Magis of the London Order. I don't know whether it was a spell or a fluke in nature or a deal with the devil, but I've always been able to shift even with mixed blood."

"It might be why you feel more comfortable fightin' in the form of a man than a hawk," Jaxx says. "You've got powerful human blood in your veins."

"Maybe. Either that or I just like guns."

Jaxx chuckles. "There's that too."

"How much magic do you have?" I ask. "And what is Lukas to you—because he's more than a driver and a bodyguard."

Kotah and Calli come into the lounge area fresh from the

shower. Both of them have damp hair and a loose-limbed swagger in their step.

"Lukas is a Squire of the London Order. He tracked me down over a decade ago and claimed he was duty-bound to serve me because of my mom. At first, I brushed him off but he made it quite clear he wouldn't allow my stubborn independence to dishonor him or his family. He's been with me ever since."

"And your powers?" I repeat. Jaxx, Calli, and Kotah all look at me and I shrug. "What? You guys can't tell me you're not interested."

"No. It's a good question," Hawk says, brushing off the scowling faces. "Part of us aligning for battle is knowing the strengths and weaknesses of one another. For example, I didn't realize Brant can't swim until I suggested dropping him in the Hudson. Those are need-to-know details."

Jaxx chuckles and heads over to the little kitchenette. "Oh, I feel a drinkin' game comin' on."

Calli and Kotah brighten and I have to admit, Jaxx's games are usually inspired and lead to a great deal of drunken mayhem. "What have you got in mind, Jaguar?"

He checks on the lasagna and closes things up again. "A Stanton version of drink and strip Never Have I Ever."

"I don't know how to play," Kotah says, "but you said drink and strip in the same sentence, so I'm in."

"That's the spirit, Wolf," Jaxx says, pouring a mishmash of ingredients into the blender we bought for the Montclair house.

"Except, I think Calli and I are at a distinct disadvantage for the stripping part."

I eye up the two of them and chuckle. Kotah's got a pair of pajama pants riding low on his hips and Calli's wearing one of Jaxx's t-shirts. As much as I love seeing her in mine, Jaxx's ride about six inches higher on her thighs, and those six inches make a big difference.

She might have underwear on, but if we're lucky, maybe not. "Yeah, you two are naked in one round."

Jaxx grins tossing me a stack of plastic cups and coming over with the blender pitcher. "Sucks to be you. Works out well for us though."

CHAPTER SIXTEEN

Calli

Jaxx's drinking game is—as usual—a riotous fun time. I'm naked by the third pledge of Never Have I Ever quint edition, but Kotah lasts way longer than any of us expect. I guess it pays to have an over-protective family to never have the freedom to do anything. Between that and him being a virgin when we got together, never had he ever done a lot of things.

In the end, though, the drinking takes hold and we need to break for lasagna or we'll be tanked and ill rather than tipsy. This is an icebreaker event, not the grand finale.

That will come later.

"Ohmygoodness that lasagna smells amazing." I close my eyes and draw the scent of tomato and garlic deep into my lungs. My stomach growls and I swallow. "I'm not going to be able to move if I eat as much of that as I want to."

Jaxx chuckles as he pulls the pan out of the oven and sets it on the stovetop to set for a few minutes while it cools. "Carbs are good for stamina."

"In about five hours."

Jaxx waggles his brow. "Sounds about right. That's when we'll start runnin' out of steam."

My voice cracks as laughter bubbles up my throat. "You're kidding right?"

Hawk hugs me from behind and kisses my temple. "Yes, he's kidding."

"Mostly," Jaxx says.

"Mostly," Hawk agrees. "Although, you are exactly right about how good that smells. Your mother is amazing."

Jaxx beams and starts cutting through the cheese with a long, serrated knife. "She is."

"Did she work the whole time you grew up?" Kotah holds a plate up to get dished a chunk of lasagna and when Jaxx sets a square of piping hot ambrosia into the center, he hands it to Brant and grabs another plate to repeat.

"No. She was home with us until we went to high school. Then she went back. She is the rolemodel of the female who can do it all."

"I hope I'm half as good at things as she is," I say.

Kotah hands me a plate and smiles. "You don't need to worry about being Mama. You're Calli and get to be on a tier all your own. Besides, research and history isn't your thing."

"That's true. Though I found the info she put together for me about the fae who might be able to contact me through the veil of the two realms quite fascinating. There are so many kinds of fae I didn't know about."

Brant nods. "Yeah, I'm curious to see what the StoneHaven side looks like."

I grab a wedge of cheesy bread and head to the little table to sit with Kotah. "Me too. According to the info Mama printed out for me on the ancient fae races on the StoneHaven side, there are three or maybe four races that could talk to me from over there. As far as she could tell, none of them could physically be on this side, though."

Hawk sits on the couch with Brant and eats off his plate on his lap. "The way I see it, there are two possibilities to explain that. Either, she was physically in this realm and is an immortal and resurrected back at a point of origin in StoneHaven, or she used some form of astral projection combined with possession to inhabit a person on this side and when that host body was killed, she retreated to her true form in the other realm."

I swallow. "You think she was some kind of fae body-snatcher? That seems harsh. It also doesn't sound like Riley."

"Not necessarily a body-snatcher. You said Riley had been a junkie street kid before you met her, right?"

"Yeah, but she cleaned up good when we got together."

"So, what if fae Riley knew that the girl she was going to possess was as good as dead and interceded. Then she wouldn't have ended her life, she assumed it."

"Are there fae races that can know stuff like that?"

Hawk nods. "Yeah. Not as a race trait but as a magic ability. The crass term for people who can do this is a mind-slut, but it's a combination of prophesizing and tethering a projected identity into a host body."

"Why would she want to do that? Why would someone from StoneHaven mind-slut herself into a street junkie to live on the streets with me for the better part of a decade?"

Jaxx brings the pan around for seconds. I take a half piece of lasagna and no bread. The boys each take another round of both. When everyone has topped up again, Jaxx digs into his second piece. "Well, if the person you're describin' did have prophesizin' abilities, could she have known Calli would be the phoenix? Could she have been protectin' her and maybe groomin' her?"

They look to me for my thoughts. "I have no idea."

"It sorta makes sense," Brant says, finishing his second piece and heading over to the counter for a third. "You said she signed you up for every self-defense class imaginable, and she kept you away from drugs, and she was devoted to you from the first moment she found you and took you in."

I shrug. "But then why not possess someone with a house and money so we didn't have to claw our way through life?"

"I can answer that." Hawk accepts a beer from Brant as the bear returns to his seat. "From my own experience, I learned a lot more about myself and what I could endure from the years I clawed through life. Being a survivor is one of the biggest advantages you've had in all this phoenix rising stuff."

I set down my cutlery and push away from the little table. "Maybe. I guess we won't know for sure until we open the gate."

Jaxx goes around the room gathering the utensils and holding out the garbage bag for our paper plates. "One thing I'm sure about, whoever or whatever Riley is, she kept you alive and strong until we found each other. I'll be forever in her debt for that."

"Abso-fucking-lutely," Hawk says, holding his beer into the air to toast me. "She gave us you, Spitfire."

Hawk

Brant and I are on cleanup from dinner while Kotah takes a midnight run to check our perimeter and Jaxx takes Calli in to rub her down with his massage oils he set out earlier.

"This is nice, eh?" Brant says, putting away the last of the cutlery and hanging the dishtowel over the handle of the little stove. "The five of us being alone in the world for a bit. Nobody knocking on the door. No cellphones buzzing. Just us talking and spending time."

I nod. "It's as awe-inspiring to me as it is foreign. I never would've guessed I could be so content hanging around naked with people and doing nothing but spending time with them."

"And enjoying one helluva sexy view."

"Well, yeah—there's that. But even when we're all dressed and shooting the shit... I don't know that I've been content. There's always been something inside me racing or chasing and I never relaxed with anyone as I do with you four. *That* is more of a shock to my system than anything."

Brant spends an inordinate amount of time adjusting the dishcloth and I get the distinct impression his mind is elsewhere. When he turns to face me and I get an eyeful of what's doin' with that monster cock of his, I'm sure of it. "Something on your mind, Bear?"

He looks me up and down and then smiles as my cock thickens and responds to the attention. Easing closer, he wraps a hand around my hip and cops a feel of my ass. Pulling us together, groin to groin, he clears his throat. "What we did the other night —the way we were together—was that only the emotion of the day and you needing to complete the bond with me?"

Ouch. "Is that the way it felt to you? I thought our hours of play were rather spectacular."

"Oh, I did too. Hands-down one of the two most memorable sextathalon nights of my life. I just wanted to check-in, you know? To tell you it was more than that to me. You rocked my foundation, Hawk. I never would've thought it was possible, but you did."

I slide my hand against his neck and into his hair, pulling his mouth to mine. His bear growls and he crushes me against the edge of the counter, the strength of his hips bending me to his will. His tongue penetrates my mouth in a seductive sweep and the growl of his bear's hunger vibrates between us.

The bus door opens behind us and Kotah trots up the steps and seals us back inside. "Sorry. I didn't mean to interrupt."

I catch my breath but don't allow Brant to pull away. If he's looking for reassurance, I'm happy to give it to him. "Not a problem, Wolf. How does everything look out there?"

"All good. We are all still alone in the great outdoors."

"Just the way we like it." When Brant moves to step away, I hold his wrist and keep him in place. "Jaxx and Calli are in the back playing massage parlor. If you want to join them, we'll be right in."

Kotah smiles and heads to the back of the bus.

When we're alone again, I pick things up where Brant left off. Our kiss is rough and heated with all the passion we shared not only the other night but a few moments ago. When I ease back from his mouth, I wrap my hand around his cock.

"As Kotah says, I am now holding the sacred wand of truth. So, let me assure you, nothing about the other night with you was about anything but me wanting to share my body and my lifestyle with you. That you got so keyed up about it made it even more fun. Did I get off on bringing your bear to the edge of violence... hells yeah, I did. Do I want to do it again... hells yeah, to that too. We're bonded mates, so I know you feel my lust and my connection, but what you can't sense is my heart. It beats stronger knowing you're at my side. I think you're brave and funny and sexy as fuck. I'm proud to call you my mate and look forward to every moment we spend together naked or otherwise."

Brant swallows but before he can speak, I shift down his body. "You got me off so good the other night, I figure I owe you a return of the favor."

"I don't think so. You got me off a dozen times more."

"Who's counting." I suck Brant's cock into my mouth, amazed again at what a big boy he is. The solid shaft is warm and salty as I slide my tongue down his length. He gasps and I take hold of him with my hand and recede to the tip. I force the tip of my tongue into the slit at the top and play. I like this myself and by the shudder of his hips, Brant's a fan too.

"Can I fuck your mouth?"

"Mhmm." I smile, remembering how much I liked that answer this morning with Calli.

"And when I come, do you want to swallow or should I pull out."

I suck off the tip of his crown with a *pop* and cast him a lascivious grin. "Oh, I eat my cream. If I make it, I claim it."

"Fuuuuck, you say the sweetest things."

I suck him back into my mouth and twist his sac. He thrusts his hips forward and I take him to the back of my throat. Grabbing the olive oil off the counter, I hand it to Brant and hold my hand out.

He doesn't hesitate. He unscrews the lid and pours a generous puddle onto my awaiting fingers.

Reaching between his legs and up, I play with his sac and glide over the smooth skin behind. When I get to where I'm going, I moisten the tight flesh of his ass and slide my middle finger inside him.

"Oh, that's good." Brant's breathy gasp cranks me up and I suck on him like I might devour him completely. Who knows, maybe I will.

Working inside him, I flick my finger forward and rub the fleshy bulge of his prostate.

"Oh... fuck, yes. That," he gasps, his hips picking up speed. "Lots of that."

I brace myself against the counter as the strength of his bear seeps into our play. With Kotah, it didn't matter how hard he fucked into my mouth, I still had strength over him. With Brant, that's not the case. Brant's bear has the raw strength to hurt me if I'm not paying attention. But I am paying attention. I'm paying very close attention.

Stimulating his pleasure with my finger and sucking him off

with long wet pulls of my mouth, it doesn't take him long before hot streams of cum coat the back of my throat.

Fuck. I don't know what it is about his cream that I find so fucking delicious. I enjoy Kotah's and Jaxx's too but there's some chemical reaction with Brant's release that is the food of the gods for me.

Too soon, Brant's body softens and his heaving breaths slow. "Thanks for that."

I wipe the dishtowel over my mouth and meet his mouth for a kiss. "My pleasure. I mean that, Bear. I'm fucking in this thing with you. It's not an obligation and you're not a means to an end. You and me, we've got something going on."

He smiles and shrugs those big shoulders of his. "I'm irresistible. What can I say."

The feminine cries of orgasm have us both looking toward the back of the bus. "Sounds like we're late to the party. We better get in there and catch up."

Brant's smile is as cocky as it is sexy. "I'm already warmed up, thanks to my fluffer."

I smack his naked ass as he saunters ahead of me toward the bedroom. "I am more than a fluffer. I'm part of the main attraction."

Brant's laughter is deep and fills the air. "Yeah, you are."

CHAPTER SEVENTEEN

Calli

I'm still riding out Kotah's release when Brant and Hawk come into the back room of the bus. They see the two of us in the center of the bed, Kotah's hands still fondling my breasts as I straddle his hips.

Brant lets off a catcall whistle. "I like it. I like it. But it's missing something... oh, me."

I giggle as Brant bounces onto the mattress, his playful side locked firmly in place. "Since Jaxx had you in here for a half-hour before any of us, I'm guessing he's taken his liberties and was mate one.

Jaxx chuckles from where he's sitting in the chair beside the bed stroking himself. "Yes sir. I only give happy endin' massages."

He nods and his dark curls flop around his face. "And our beloved wolf here has made his contribution to the night's endeavor now too?"

Kotah nods. "I have."

Brant sits back on his knees and smiles. "Wolf, are you good to take a back seat if I tag in and want to ride our beautiful female up front?"

"I'm good for anything," Kotah says. "Where do you want me?"

"Stay there, we'll just make some orifice adjustments. You game, Calli?"

I chuckle as he lifts me off Kotah and spins me reverse cowgirl to face Kotah's feet instead of his face. Brant sets me on my knees and kneels in front of me. Reaching between my legs, he plays in the remnants of both Jaxx's and Kotah's releases soaking my core. "Nice, so I see slide and glide won't be an issue."

"You're welcome," Jaxx says, still keeping a lazy round of rub and tug going.

"Thank you, Jaguar. You too, Wolf. Though, you're not done yet, Kotah. Up and at it, my man." Brant palms Kotah's sated and soft cock and wakes it back to life. "Lovely assistant, glove his love and lube me up."

He holds his hand out flat toward Hawk. Our avian is on the job and squeezes out a glop of lube.

"Thank you, sir. I'm just going to..." he reaches beneath me and gets me primed for anal. "Wolf, are you set?"

Kotah tosses the empty condom packet onto the bedside table and props up his cock. "All set."

Brant smiles. "Then, if you would... and if your wood would."

"Oh, his wood, would," Jaxx says, tipping his head to the side to watch as I descend inch by delectable inch onto Kotah. "Yeehaw."

Calli, lay back on our wolf and get comfy."

I do as I'm told and recline so I'm lying on top of Kotah. My back is on his chest and he wraps his arms around me in a tender embrace. I turn my face to meet Kotah's kiss. "Hey, sweet prince. You good?"

"Hey back," he says, gripping my hips and thrusting up from underneath. "I'm great."

Brant crawls up our joined bodies and it's a good thing he's tall and broad because I don't think anyone else would still be able to come inside me like this. "Close your eyes, beautiful, and absorb the sense of being filled."

Usually taking Brant in is a stretch to the point of plea-sured-pain, tonight it's not. Either I'm stretched, relaxed, and super wet from Kotah and Jaxx, or he's had a release or two himself out in the front of the bus with Hawk and he's not as marble hard and solid. Or a combo of both.

"Is this alright, beautiful? Not too much? Not too sore?"

I smile at the worry in his voice. He's holding back until he's sure I'm good. Always does, my sweet teddy bear. "I'm good." I press my palms against the wide, chiseled planes of his chest. "I could use a little more in and out friction though. It's been a slow night."

All four of my men laugh at that.

Brant takes his time taking his pleasure. He draws his kiss down the column of my neck and across my collarbone. Then, his attention shifts, and he falls still. "Servicing Jaxx now, eh? You're gonna rival Calli soon for the title of Lover of Cock-sucking."

I open my eyes in time to see Hawk flip Brant the bird, his head bobbing over Jaxx's lap. Jaxx's head has dropped back against the cushion of the chair and his hips are flexing to greet each plunge.

"Oh, I'll battle for that title." I gasp as Brant starts moving again. "Drop the gauntlet, Barron. There can be only one."

"I stand as tribute," Kotah says.

I laugh, and then all thoughts of blowjobs abandon me as he reclaims the rounds of my breasts and tweaks my nipples. "Oh, Wolf."

The steady thrust and retreat of Brant have me riding both

his and Kotah's erections. The sensation is overwhelming, the tingle of my cells building up to one helluva climax.

"Gawd... you feel good, Bear."

"Ditto."

A long, loud purr rolls out of Jaxx and I'm sucked into watching his face as his orgasm closes in. The purr is rough and rattled and vibrates in my core. Over the past weeks, I've heard his animal sounds enough to know his finish is closing in fast.

The *slap, slap, slap* of flesh on flesh grows louder and faster and I groan as erotic pleasure zings from the tips of my nipples straight to my core. "Gawd, that sound. You're gonna make me come, Jaxx."

"Me too," Kotah breathes beneath me.

"Me three," Brant says, pumping harder. "That sound triggers my cock to spill every damned time."

I don't know if Jaxx even hears us. His eyes are pinched shut and he's got both hands clutched around Hawk's head pumping him into his lap.

The purr is still going strong and it calls to my phoenix. Of all of them, Jaxx brings the wild forward in me the most. He calls my animal and I've stopped trying to control it.

My phoenix is ascending. She's strong and possessive and so fucking turned on by her mates it's indescribable. Fire ignites in my core and my eyes flip open.

Brant's gaze locks on mine and he gasps. "Oh, fuck."

On a shout, he pitches his hips forward and locks into place. With bruising fingers at my hips, he thrusts forward, releasing into me. I ride out the breathy grunts as he topples off the cliff of control.

As always with them, I feel the streams of heat and groan as my orgasm takes hold. I swallow and try to hold off, but with the air smelling like sex and their throaty grunts filling my ears, my hips convulse and my world shatters.

I cry out, arching above Kotah's chest even as he comes

inside me from below. His chest heaves in and out, his heart pounding against my back.

Even though I've had three of them multiple times already tonight, my phoenix isn't finished. I am hunger and want. I am missing one of my mates and ache with the need of having him inside me.

"Hawk," I say, in a voice that's not my own. "I need you to complete this. Your phoenix needs her fourth."

Hawk

At the call of my name, I turn from swallowing Jaxx's cream and my mouth falls open. Brant is easing out of Calli and something monumental has changed since I sucked Jaxx into my mouth. Calli's glistening wet and the scent of our mixed arousals and emissions is thick in the air. But what's more incredible than the sensory overload is the female herself.

"Holy fuck."

"Yep," Brant says, still staring. "My reaction too."

"Hawk, take me. Now!" she says.

Brant winces. "I say you do what she says and fuck her."

I'm of two minds on that. One, holy fuck, Calli is more wildling than female at the moment and two, if the scary mythical bird that is your mated wife needs you to fuck her—then you climb the glowing fire beast female and you do as you're told.

Calli flaps her wings and rises off Kotah, leaving the other three with mirrored expressions caught between awe, terror, and lust. I'm with them. Our mate resembles her female aflame in size and form, but she's got wings. And though she's glowing gold, there's no flame coming off her.

She's more like a bird goddess.

"And I thought you couldn't get any sexier," Jaxx says.

"Resplendant," Kotah says.

"I'm still stuck on holy fuck," Brant adds.

"Hawk, I hunger and wait," her voice vibrates through me and seems to pinball between my cock and balls, firing my adrenaline into overdrive.

Right. I give my head a shake and take a quick assessment. Yep. She still has all the right parts and pieces to get this mating bond completed. I've never been at a loss for what to do with a naked female, but as Brant says, holy fuck.

With a thrust of her wings, she closes the distance between me and the bed and wraps herself around me. Her legs grapple my hips and her arms clutch my shoulders. It's the contact of our bodies and the connection of our mating bond that brings things back into focus.

This is still Calli. Somehow, inside this golden goddess fire beast, our mate is coming into her own.

"You amaze me every fucking day, Spitfire." I push her up against the built-in armoire against the wall. With her upper body pinned to the wooden doors, I reach below her thighs and guide myself into the soaked folds of her cunny. "Man, you're so wet."

The moment I'm inside her, the current of power coming off of her jolts my junk like I'm plugged into a power receptacle. "And your cells are alive with power."

"I feel strong." She flips her head back, her hair blowing out behind her like she's a supermodel in a fashion shoot. "Take me to the bed and lay me down."

I do as she commands and lay her back on the tousled sheets of the bed. Her hair fans out against the black backdrop like golden rays of the sun. I grip the top ridge of her wings as leverage and continue to rock inside her.

Her eyes roll closed and her lips turn up in a smile. "I want all of you. Kotah and Brant, I want your mouths and your cocks.

Jaxx, I've waited long enough to see you and Hawk joined and working up a sweat. Take him while he takes me."

Jaxx's brow arches in question as he meets my gaze. I give him the go-ahead and he nods. "Yes ma'am."

My jaguar climbs onto the bed behind me and I focus on Calli. If I get all up in my head about Jaxx topping me in front of the others, my hawk will get panicky and balk. It'll be fine. Jaxx will make sure of that. I trust him to know—

I tense as his ministrations bring the drip and glide of lubrication into play but let myself get mesmerized by the flames flickering and dancing around the pupils of Calli's eyes. It's a haunting sight but amazing at the same time.

"You good, hotness?" Jaxx's voice is tender and quiet and soothes my anxiety even more.

"Yeah. Go for it."

Calli's got a grip on both Kotah and Brant. They're on their knees on either side of her head and she's stroking them.

Jaxx is right where I want him and even though this is more public than we've ever been, I remind myself that everything is as it should be. These are my mates. Whatever the alpha, dom, kingpin of the fae world hangups I've got, they don't apply here. I am safe.

The penetration brings that stammer in my heart that I love so much. I drop my head against Calli's neck and absorb that first glorious glide to fill me.

"So hot," Calli says.

I push up on my palms and claim her mouth, my tongue matching the push and invade of Jaxx's actions. After a few minutes of gauging the situation, our jaguar gets down to it. I groan as servicing me morphs into pounding. I broaden my arms and dig my palms deep into the mattress to brace myself.

With each succulent *smack, smack, smack,* of his hips hitting my ass, I'm rammed deeper inside Calli. She's loving it, writhing underneath me her breath picking up speed.

"Give me your legs, kitten. Let me open you wider for Hawk's cock."

Calli moans and lifts her feet into the air. Jaxx grips her legs at the back of her knees and leverages his hold to pull the three of us tighter together with each hammering stroke.

"Oh, yeah," Jaxx gasps, behind me. "That's good."

Good. I'm completely pinned in Calli's clenching depths with my wild and wonderful lover taking me rough from behind. As much as I'd love to claim Calli's mouth, Jaxx's rhythm is too punishing for anything beyond holding on for the ride of a lifetime.

Our love before me... Our passion behind.

Brant barks a curse and spills jets of ropey cream over Calli's hand and down her arm. Kotah's next and it's the same thing. Our wolf arches back, paying Calli homage. The power building in our phoenix spikes and her orgasm shatters her.

The magic of the mating bond explodes. It ignites in my cells, spreading through my body like a brush fire in August. It's hot and sharp and there's no fighting my release.

Heat erupts from my sac and I press hard into my mate and give her everything I've got. The muscles in my neck strain tight as I shout, caught in the vortex of the complete unlocking of Calli's phoenix.

Jaxx must feel it too because he comes hard, the feral roar of his cat filling the sex-saturated air of the bus stateroom. The sound is wild and calls my hawk forward.

The world spins and there's an explosion. I'm knocked off the bed and land in a tangle of arms and legs with Jaxx. Before I can roll to my knees, my hawk ascends and I search the room through the eyes of my wildling form. Jaxx's jaguar roars beside me, his cat's turquoise gaze locked on the bed.

Calli's phoenix goddess is ebbing power, her golden form pulsing with magical energy. She's too fucking inspiring for words. She flaps her wings and rises out of a gaping hole in the roof of the bus.

That must've been the explosion.

I push off, flapping my wings, and follow her out past the curled metal and into the night sky. The roar of Brant's bear tells me what I already know.

Wherever Calli's going, our mates can't follow.

CHAPTER EIGHTEEN

Calli

$\mathcal{A}$ cool breeze blowing over my bare ass wakes me with a jolt. Where am I? I sit up and study my surroundings. I'm alone in a wooded thicket and completely naked. The sun is almost at its zenith, so I've been here for a long time, but I don't know much more than that.

Where are my mates? The last thing I remember is Hawk and Brant joining Jaxx, Kotah, and I in the bus bedroom.

My mind is fumbling through the fog of last night when the shriek of a massive raptor brings my gaze skyward. I raise my hand to shield my eyes as Hawk swoops down, through the canopy of the trees.

In his talons, he's gripping a ball of blue plaid which he drops beside me before landing gracefully as a man. "You're awake. How are you feeling?"

"Confused. Where are we? And what the hell are you wearing?"

He pulls up the worn, jean overalls he's wearing and sits on the ground beside me. "Desperate times breed desperate measures, mate. I can only manifest the clothes I had on when I turned hawk. I was nakey, so I had to improvise." He unfurls the blue plaid to offer me a man's flannel shirt. "And to answer your other question, not far from Peoria, Illinois."

"Why are we here?" He helps me into the shirt and I'm thankful to feel at least slightly less exposed. I give it the sniff test. Though it's used, at least it's clean.

"I was hoping you'd know the answer to that question. After we completed the mating ritual, your phoenix goddess persona blew off the top of the bus and flew away. I followed you and this is where you landed to take a sleep."

"Phoenix goddess persona?"

Hawk goes on to explain to me how I transitioned into a new evolution of myself and how they found me both stunningly sexy as well as slightly terrifying at the same time.

"I don't remember that."

"I'm not surprised," he says, lounging back on a patch of grass. "When our wildling sides ascend fully the first couple of times, no one remembers much."

"Where are the others?"

"Hopefully, on their way here to meet us. We left naked. I didn't have money or any way to get in touch with them. Since we're using brand-new burner phones, I don't have their numbers even if I did have my phone."

"So, what do we do?"

"I called Lukas. He has the burner numbers because he bought them. He'll call them and tell them where to find us."

"How long will that take?"

"Well, I called him a couple of hours ago and it's likely a five-hour drive, so I'm guessing we have a few hours until they get here."

"If there's a town around here, I can teach you how to panhandle for a burger. I'm starving."

Hawk flashes me with a look so beyond shocked I bust up laughing.

"Or I can show you the best places to dumpster dive but I figured you'd rather panhandle."

"I'd rather turn into a hawk, capture, and eat a wild rabbit… which I detest, by the way."

I stand up and wipe the bits of sticks and grass off my bare thighs. "Well, if I could turn into a phoenix and catch a bacon double-cheeseburger, I would, but I can't and I'm starving. Besides, wearing only Farmer Joe's shirt, it'll be quick. Men love giving generous donations to pretty damsels in distress."

"No, Calli." Hawk stomps behind me as I wander through the trees. "No mate of mine, male or female, will ever beg for food. Not as long as blood still pumps through my cold, dark heart."

I hear the genuine insult and worry in his voice and turn. "Hey, there. Don't get yourself whipped into a tizzy. It's not your job to keep me fed and clothed. That's *my* job. I appreciate everything you do for me but when the chips are down, I'm a survivor, remember?"

The *thwump, thwump, thwump* sound of rotor blades cutting through the nearby sky ends our argument. The rigid stiffness in Hawk's shoulders relaxes and he casts me a triumphant smile. "Thank the Powers. Lukas is here and this argument is moot. Come, Spitfire."

"Don't come, Spitfire me." He reaches to grab me and I pull back, still pissed.

"Calm yourself. Let me get you a—" He tries again to grab me and I yank my arm back. The movement pulls him off balance he stumbles forward. The sudden shift in position puts him directly in front of me as the crack of gunfire echoes through the trees.

I scream as Hawk spins behind the force of impact and collapses to the forest floor.

My phoenix bursts forward and I shriek, blowing a stream of flame at the direction from which the shot came. Gunfire rends the air and I hold out my wings to shield Hawk. Do these assholes think they can take my mate from me?

Think again.

There's no way I can navigate through the trees when I'm fifteen feet tall and have a wingspan of thirty feet. To do anything, I'll have to fly straight up and out of the trees and leave Hawk.

Can I clear our path and get him to safety?

The scent of his blood in the air is testing my control. Do I grab him and run or protect him and fight? I don't know.

Fight, girlfriend. Riley says in my head. *Always fight.*

Unsure if my bestie is here with me now or if my subconscious is burping up the answer she always gave me, I go with my gut. Pivoting on a slow turn, I spew fire and create a wall of flames around Hawk.

When the wall of fire is lit and rising twenty feet from the forest floor, I push off to face whatever these assholes think they have in store for us.

I push through the canopy of the thicket and launch straight up at the blazing sun. The heat of the fiery star feeds my power and I arch in the air and dive backward to loop back around to face whoever is stupid enough to come at me.

I spot the helicopter first and tuck my wings back, dropping into a full dive. Shrieking my fury, I bolster my heat and slam to the ground, stomping on their stupid metal bird.

The impact sends a shockwave into the ground and the fuel tanks explode around me. Nothing touches me. I'm living magma. Everything that comes near me melts before contact.

As their means of escape goes up in flames, men yell and scramble. They're still trying to shoot me with their weapons. Puny idiots. I scream and scorch them where they stand.

I recognize the sound of the rocket launcher the moment it

fires. I turn and bat away the incoming missile, sending it straight into the ground fifty feet away.

The guy holding the launcher goes from being all brash and ballsy to realizing he just pissed off the wrong fiery bitch in two seconds flat. I flap my wings and launch, gripping him with my talons and popping him like a bug.

Screaming with the fury of feeling Hawk's pain through our bond, I lay waste to everyone still moving. The blaze is wild and burning hotter than mere flame.

It's burning at phoenix flame temperature.

With the enemy taken care of, I push into the air, find the ring of flames protecting Hawk, and land beside him.

He looks bad. The bullet hit his back and tore its way through his chest. I don't have to call my tears, they flow freely seeing him in this state. I tip my head to the side and rest my beak down his legs. Blinking a couple of times, I deposit my tears directly into his wound.

With one final shriek, I pick up my mate and fly straight into the solid rays of the midday sun.

Jaxx

It's close to four o'clock in the afternoon when I pull the bus to the side of the road where Lukas told us to meet Hawk and Calli. "Guys, you need to come up here and see this."

Kotah and Brant have been pacing for hours but unlike when we have Hawk's jet and helicopter handy, the bus doesn't just sweep us up and take us where we want to go—no matter how badly we want it.

"What the fuck is all this." Brant bends to scowl out the front windshield.

"I guess we need to go and find out." I shut things down and swing open the door of the bus. There are a dozen state trooper cars, a couple of fire trucks, and a coroner van. "It can't be good, whatever it is."

My cat is prowling and growling inside me and I try to ease him back.

"There's Lukas." Kotah points into the sea of uniforms. As if alerted by the mention of his name, Lukas turns from the charred skeleton of a mangled helicopter and jogs over.

"Where are they?" Brant asks, the second Hawk's right-hand man arrives. "Because we can feel when our mates are close and they aren't."

"But they're not dead?" Lukas asks.

My cat growls. "Why is that your first question?"

He checks over his shoulder and we move away from the bustle of the scene. "When I spoke to Barron earlier, I told him I would give you the message about where they were and meet you all here. He suspected that since the final mating was complete and Calli's powers were unlocked her phoenix was drawn to the site of the Portal Gate. He wanted me to arrange a team and join you five so we could all go in together."

"But?"

"But when I got here, there was a blown-up helicopter, twelve men fried extra-crispy, and a blast zone the size of a football field."

I turn to Kotah and Brant and tip my head toward the trees. "Circle the back of the trees and see if your wolf can scent anythin'. Brant, you go with him and stop anyone from shootin' the wolf if he gets spotted."

The two of them nod and jog off.

I sigh, an uneasy tension building in my chest. "I don't like this. What do the locals think happened?"

Lukas shrugs. "A couple of farmers said they saw a flaming bird and an explosion. The troopers are chalking that up to the helicopter being on fire as it crash-landed and exploded."

"And the twelve men?"

"There are a couple of trucks further up the road that we think are connected. They're thinking there was a gathering of men for some unknown purpose and the chopper came in hot. The explosion caused a brush fire and the men were trapped and perished."

"That's a stretch."

Lukas shrugs. "Honestly, I don't care. It's plausible and the human authorities are buying it, so good for them."

"And what's your take on things?"

Lukas frowns. "I don't think they're far off. I think the two truckloads of men were scouts and confirmed that Calli and Hawk were here. They likely either spotted her flying in last night or saw some random social media post about a shooting comet flaming across the Missouri sky. Whatever their intel, they discovered Calli here, and sent a tactical team in to remove her from the equation."

"And only Hawk to defend her."

"Or not. When I spoke to him, he'd left her unconscious in a thicket of woods. He said she'd been out for hours and he needed to steal some clothes and rally us to join them. Maybe the Black Knight's men found her when she was sleeping. Maybe they tried to take her by force."

"I don't think so." Brant jogs back from the trees with Kotah. "Tell them, buddy."

Kotah captures his hair and ties it back. "There's a ring of scorched earth deeper in the trees and at the center of it, the ground is thick with the scent of Hawk's blood."

I curse, my stomach squirreling. "You're sure?"

He nods. "Yeah. My wolf knows what each of your blood smells like after the past six weeks. I'm sure."

"So, Hawk's hurt and there are bad guy's coming at them," Brant says. "Our girl encases Hawk in a cone of flames and takes them out with her fiery phoenix fury."

I nod. "That would be my guess."

"Then where are they?" Lukas says, scanning the skyline. "And why is the top of the tour bus blown out like an exploded popcorn kernel?"

"It's our new moon roof," Brant says. "It's right above the bed so we can see the stars. Very romantic."

I roll my eyes. "Not the best if it rains though."

Brant chuckles. "No. I suppose not."

Lukas grabs a walkie off his belt and presses the long bar on the side. "Mackie, come to the bus by the road." Then he looks at us. "Go inside, grab what you need, and meet me at the helicopter. I'll have Mackie drive the bus to the next town for repair. I figure our best bet of catching up with two birds is to be airborne."

Brant snorts. "Ha, catching two birds with one copter."

I turn and point them toward the bus. "Clean up anything private. Grab our files and our go-bags. Oh, and Hawk's fifty grand. No sense leaving it behind for the repairmen to find."

Kotah nods and he and Brant head off to get us packed.

When it's just the two of us, I turn to Lukas and frown. "He's not dead. I feel him through our bond. And, if he's hurt, there's no one better for him to be stranded with than Calli. His best chance of survival is her cryin' for him."

Lukas nods. "That was my take on things too."

"But logically, if they got away and she was able to heal him well enough to get to a phone... well, if everythin' was hunkydory, he would've contacted us by now."

Lukas lets off a heavy sigh. "Agreed."

"So that begs the question... where the hell are they?"

Hawk

Three things become clear to me from the moment I regain consciousness. One: Once Calli's phoenix crushed the troops that came to kill her, she healed me with her tears and flew me somewhere her wildling side felt safe. Two: The place she felt safe is very high up on a rocky ledge about four hundred feet in the air. Three: With her now in human form, there's no way for her to get down.

With neither of us eating or drinking in close to seventeen hours, she doesn't have the strength to transform again without a solid night's sleep and fueling up on another of Mama's lasagna feasts.

"Calli?" I press a probing hand against my chest and finding nothing but the faintest ache. I'm naked again. The fire of Calli's phoenix doesn't burn any of us, but it's hell on clothing. Oh well, I wasn't keen on those overalls anyway. "Spitfire? Are you okay?"

She stirs beside me and I reach forward to protect her from rolling close to the edge of the jagged ledge. She's naked and shivering and my heart lurches inside my ribs to see her so exhausted. "Oh, my love. We need to get us both some clothes and find help."

When she doesn't rouse more than stirring and a quiet groan, the hair on the nape of my neck stands on end. "Calli, wake up for me. Let me see those emerald green eyes."

I shift on the rocky ledge, the jagged surface scratching my legs. The ledge itself is wide enough to hold Calli when she was in her full phoenix form, so it's not tiny, but it's too high up to feel comfortable moving around if she's not fully alert. I scoop her off the stone, move her back to the rockface, and settle her into my lap.

"What's wrong baby? Is it a lack of food and too much exertion? Are you hurt?"

I brush my hands over her body, rolling her forwards and back to check for injury. There are none.

"Good. That's good."

Her body trembles as a shiver racks her and I pull her closer, rubbing my hands over her flesh. "Did you use up all your heat? I guess I'll have to keep you warm then, yeah?"

I look out at the land and wonder where the hell we are now. If I am right about her being drawn toward the gate, my guess is we're somewhere between Peoria, Illinois, and Lebanon, Kansas.

When all the portals to StoneHaven were removed and destroyed, only the one at the continental center of the United States was preserved. Hidden in a crag in what is now considered one of the local bouldering sites for the state, the humans remain oblivious to the portal held within.

"Calli? If I lay you down away from the edge of the ledge, would you promise not to roll off if I take a very quick look around?"

The grumbling moan I get in return doesn't comfort me. I don't want to leave her, but I'm worried about her going into shock. In some cases, wildling transitioning for some of the larger, more dominant species can take too much out of the host side. Calli turning into a phoenix counts as being the largest and most dominant species of our race.

"You said you were starving earlier and that was hours ago. You must be famished now, eh?" Okay, that gives me an idea. I could hunt for a rabbit or a mouse or something for her to eat. If she could muster up a fire, we could cook it.

I take in her current condition and curse. She's not mustering up any fire anytime soon. "Okay, not that then."

The sun is still pretty high over the horizon, so I figure it's maybe five or six o'clock. "Brant, Kotah, and Jaxx would've arrived at the thicket a couple of hours ago. They'll be looking for us by now. They've assessed the carnage at the site and are working with Lukas to find us. How do we help them find us, Spitfire?"

Her head lolls to the side and I prop it against my shoulder and finger through her hair. "You rest. I don't want you to slip into a coma due to system shutdown. I'll get you fed and rested and warmed up somehow. I'll think of something. I always do."

I press a kiss to her forehead and will my strategic mind to come up with something brilliant. How do I let Jaxx and the others know where we are?

~

Brant

My bear is pacing like a wild beast inside me and I'm losing hold on my tether. "She's not good. Something's wrong."

Jaxx nods, rubbing his chest. "I know. I feel it too."

"Is it the Black Knight?" Lukas asks. "Have they been captured? Is she injured?"

"No," Jaxx says, picking a different path than me to pace around the helicopter. "It's not that. She's just..."

"Fading," Kotah says. Our wolf is sitting cross-legged in the field we landed in. "Her strength is waning and her fire is dim."

Lukas runs a rough hand over his face. "Well, there's a fuck-ton of space between that thicket of burnt trees and the Portal Gate in Kansas. If we keep flying, we're just as likely to pass them and be too far out of the way. We need something to go on."

"Don't you think we fucking know that?" I snap, stomping forward. My claws extend past the nailbeds of my fingers and my bear growls with the need to lash out and shred someone. "Don't you think we've run through every scenario to find a way to get to them? They're our fucking mates."

Jaxx steps between me and the military man and flashes me a look. "Take five, Bear. Lukas is worried and tryin' to help. He wants Hawk and Calli safe too."

"It's too bad Hawk's not still chipped," Kotah says. "At least then we could've tracked him."

Lukas chuffs. "In the future, maybe I should chip all of you again. It would make my job so much easier. The five of you never sit still."

I stretch my neck from side to side. "Okay, we aren't chipped, but we are bound. Kotah, are you getting anything we can use on the mating bond?"

"I can feel them, but no, the bond tells us the connectedness of our mates and that, in turn, tells us about the health and well-being of them. It doesn't pinpoint where they are in any way."

"What if they have sex?" Jaxx asks. "We can always feel it when two of us are goin' at it. Do you think we'd be able to track them that way?"

"No," I shake that off. "When you and Hawk were in Vancouver, we knew you were going at it but we didn't get any indication of where you were. There was nothing like that coming through the bond."

"Then how do we find them?" Kotah asks.

"We don't," Jaxx says, frowning. "There's not a damned thing we can do until Hawk or Calli can contact us. No matter how much it sucks. Our hands are tied."

CHAPTER NINETEEN

Hawk

$\mathcal{I}$ drop the sticks and dried brush I've collected onto the pile and swoop back around to descend to the cliff ledge. Transforming to man, I land on my feet and check on Calli lying too still against the rockface. "Well, we are officially in the middle of nowhere, my love. If there is any life around here it's too far and I'd be away from you too long."

Gathering the dried wood and detritus, I settle in to make a fire. Hopefully, if I can raise her body temperature, I can ignite a flame in her and maybe call her phoenix.

Setting the little pile of sticks into a tent, I place the bits of dried scrub beneath and grab the two sticks I chose to rub together to start the flame.

"Here's hoping I still remember how to do this. It's been quite a few years since I found myself needing to warm myself alone in the wilderness. Too bad we can't order a fire by take-out. That could be a new business venture—we could call it Uber Heats."

I chuckle at my joke and grimace at the chatter of her teeth.

It's not that cold out. She used up all her heat to defeat my father's men and bring me here. My fucking father. He's taken so much from me, he can't take anything more.

I won't let him.

"I should've raced off and gotten you food first thing. I didn't realize it costs you so much to hold your phoenix form. I'm sorry."

Knowing I failed her, cleaves my heart in two.

When she needed sustenance, I brought her a flannel shirt. A lot of good that did.

"I flew all around this wooded section of nowherelandia and didn't see any sign of a way to get you off this ledge. If you could just open your eyes and fly down with me, I can take it from there."

I work on the fire for what feels like an eternity, but it's likely no more than an hour. My arms ache and my palms are blistered and still, not so much as a smolder. As desperate as I am to warm her, leaving her exposed on the stone while I fail at this is costing her heat.

I'm sweating like a roasted turkey in the oven, but she's still freezing. Dropping onto the rough stone beside her, I gather Calli into my arms. She makes no indication that she's aware I've moved her... or that I'm there at all.

"It's ironic, don't you think? I can't even make a spark when you're sitting right here and can breathe flames when you're awake."

During the time wasted on *not* starting a fire, the sun has gone down and the night's chill creeps over my skin now that I'm still. If Calli was cold before, the drop in temperature won't help.

"Come on, Calli," I say with more heat than I feel. "Open your eyes and help me here. You put us up on this ledge, help me get you down. Some help with the fire would be nice. Transforming would be even better. Hell, I'd take you opening your eyes and at least looking at me."

Nothing. No matter what I say, Calli isn't hearing me. Or maybe she's hearing me and being sucked deeper into whatever abyss she's stuck in.

"Don't you give up, Calli. I'll figure this out. I'll get you warm and hydrated and I'll fill your belly to bursting. If you want a bacon double cheeseburger, I'll buy you a fucking diner. We'll sit and make food and eat for the next two days."

I brush her hair back from her face and feel the shards of my heart splintering in my chest. Wildlings who suffer from things like this slip into comas and die.

It's uncommon but it happens.

The thought of that happening to her clogs my throat. I tip my head back and scream into the night to release the pressure building in my chest. My voice echoes off the stone and treed parklands below, my vocal cords straining.

Nothing eases the pain.

"Don't you *dare* die on me, Spitfire," I shout, giving her a shake. "You made me buy into this whole mating thing. You convinced me that my life could be more than it was. You can't take that away from me now. Where's the fight? Where's the female who dressed me down and met me with fire and fury every time I fucked up?"

I give her another shake but it's no use. She's a ragdoll in my arms. She brought me up here to give me a safe place to heal, so I could live. It's killing me that with everything I am and accomplished in life... I can't return the favor.

Tears sting my eyes and I bend my head over her. "Maybe if I cry for you for once, eh? Maybe that will help. I'm not much for waterworks, baby, but at this point, I haven't got anything else to offer you but a broken heart."

My fear of losing her is real and it takes root inside me. What will we do without our phoenix? The four of us will be lost. The realms will be stuck. Will the universe choose another female to take her place? The idea is repugnant.

No one could take her place. Calli is a true original.

My tears drip off my cheeks and dampen her hair. I feel the life draining out of her as her body gives in to the finality of our situation. The loss vibrates along our mating bond and then everything goes dark inside me.

How can this be possible? How can I lose her?

I gasp as my sobbing brings me to rasping breaths. "Fuck, Calli. Fight. Don't go. I've done everything you asked. I opened my mind to the possibility. I opened my heart. Now you do what I ask—wake the fuck up."

I pinch the wedding band on her finger and clasp it to the agony ripping apart my chest. "I love you, Calliope Tannis. I love your insouciance and your loyalty and your annoying, incessant quirks. We all do. Jaxx will be destroyed if you don't hang on. He'd never say so, but I know how much he wants our children. And Kotah... he'll never survive that fucking palace without you. You're his rock when life threatens to take his soul. And Brant... that oaf of a bear loves you so hard I don't think he'll ever crack wise again. You're his joy, Calli. You're all of our joy. Stay with us. Fight to find your fire."

Jaxx

I'm racing through the trees on all fours with Kotah's wolf when something shifts inside me. My skin tingles ultra-sensitive and my blood pulses fast. My cat snarls in recognition. Yeah, we've experienced this before. All the fear and anger that's been crushing me for hours lifts. This is it. If I'm right, we now have our way of finding them.

Kotah's gait is off, his wolf unsure about the strange sensation. *Right,* neither he nor Brant felt this before. It was only Hawk and me. I don't have time to explain now.

I bump his shoulder with mine and turn back to the field where Lukas and Brant are waiting at the helicopter.

Brant is pacing when we get back, a puzzled scowl etched on his face. He rubs his chest center mass and growls. "What's happening? What is this?"

"You feel it too?" asks Kotah, changing on the fly and jogging to a stop in front of him.

He dips his chin. "Where's it coming from?"

"Where's what coming from," Lukas asks.

I point to the helicopter and Brant and Kotah hop in. "It's a distant warnin' bell goin' off in the back of our minds. It happened once before when we were in North Dakota. Hawk and I sensed a change in our bond and tracked Kotah and Calli to the grotto."

"Hawk's soul shard," Kotah says.

My chest warms, and my mating crystal starts to glow through the fabric of my shirt. The three of us fish out our leather-wrapped crystal shards and hold them up for all to see. "The fourth crystal is activatin'. We need to get in the air."

Lukas nods. "Buckle up."

Hawk

My tears dry up and I'm still at a loss. Calli's breathing is slow and shallow. With my hand pressed on her chest, I measure the movement, wondering if it's slowing towards a stop or if that's my worst fear playing tricks on me.

"I love you, Calli." My words haven't completely left my lips when a flicker of light brings my gaze up to the sky. The purple velvet of night shifts and swirls in front of me, bursting into gold, green, pink, and blue.

"A little too far south for Aurora Borealis, isn't it?"

My hawk ascends as the shimmering colors drop directly in front of the ledge and advance toward us. Even with the building movement of light, the world around is swallowed up by the void of night.

As the swirling light grows closer, my mage side triggers, and I sense the fae magic. Despite my desire to hold and protect Calli, I lay her down and rise to my feet.

"I think I know what this is about," I say, hurt and annoyed that the universe waited until now to award me what's mine. "Not that my mating crystal does us much good now. It's supposed to unite the power of the quint for our phoenix, but look at her... does she look like she's in any shape to take on the Portal Gate? She gave her life for me and *now* I'm engaged enough to get my soul shard? Fuck you."

A small flash of light breaks free from the swirling color. It's brilliant and bright and I shield my eyes with my hand as it drifts closer. And, yep, hovering within the light, there it is—

My mating crystal.

I open my palm and reach over the edge of the ledge. The magical gemstone settles into my hand and my body glows with the same golden aura the others did when they first held theirs.

Golden rays radiate from me like a shockwave of pulsing energy. They extend from me and shoot across the night sky, into the darkness beyond.

If it's the same as when this happened with Kotah, those pulsing rays of energy will seek the others to complete the connection. When I close my hand around the shard, my bond with the quint locks tighter into place.

My eyes glass up again and I blink against the sting of tears. I finally, whole-heartedly belong somewhere and it's too late. I look through the moisture clouding my eyes and stare at the stone nestled in my hand.

It doesn't have the feel of swirling water like Jaxx's, like the essence of spirit, like Kotah's, or earth, like Brant's. The interior of my shard glows and swirls with the essence of air.

I take it back to where I left Calli lying against the seam of the rockface and the ledge and pull her back into my lap. Wrapping my arms around her, I pray some of the magical glow I'm rocking will warm her up.

"See, Spitfire, I told you I was all-in."

Calli

Beep... beep... beep... I fight against the drugging effect holding my eyelids shut. What happened? Where am I? Beep... beep... beep... And what's that incessant beeping?

"You guys, she's coming back to us." The dulcet tones of my sweet prince relax me a little. He squeezes my hand and pulls my knuckles up to his lips. "*Chigua*, open your eyes so my wolf can finally rest. We need to see you are well."

I swallow and my head lolls to the side. When did my noggin start weighing a thousand pounds? Likely the same time my eyelids morphed into being made of lead.

"Come on, Spitfire," Hawk says. "I've got your take-out order here. Enough bacon cheeseburgers to fill your belly to the point of exploding."

Yum. I want to respond, I do. And yeah, they smell good.

"You scared us, kitten," Jaxx whispers beside my ear. He presses a kiss to my temple and runs his lips up the side of my cheek. As he breathes in my scent, his jaguar lets off a long, content purr. "We almost lost you. Our animal sides are wild and a little dangerous right now. We need you to wake up."

I draw a deep, steadying breath and force my eyes open. My mates are here. Kotah and Jaxx at my bedsides and Hawk at the foot of my bed, standing behind a dozen, paper takeout bags. Where is Brant—there—

My bear is sitting in the corner looking haunted. He's bent over with his brawny arms propped on his knees and his eyes are as gold as I've ever seen them in his human form.

"Come here, Bear. You look like you need a hug."

His huge frame pushes into motion and he crawls onto the bed. The others scramble. Kotah barely gets out of the way fast enough. Hawk grabs the bags full of cheeseburgers and curses Brant's stupid size sixteen feet, and Jaxx grabs the plastic tube attached to my wrist and moves it out of the way as quickly as his cat reflexes can react.

The chaos settles quickly though.

Once Brant snuggles in and pulls me against his chest, the growling stops and they all seem to relax—even me.

I breathe in the worry and fear radiating off my guys and my phoenix takes offense. These men are warriors and my weakness is making them shaky.

I give Brant a bone-crushing hug—which he likely barely feels—and ease back. "Okay, I'm awake. Bring on the cheeseburgers and tell me what I missed while we fill our bellies."

Brant eases back and studies me. "Are you sure you're up for that?"

"Hells yeah, those burgers smell *soooo* good and it looks like Hawk bought enough for all of our bellies to fill to exploding. Thank you, hotness."

I take a page from Jaxx's book and borrow the endearment. Hawk seems too impersonal all the time, surly seems inaccurate now that we've broken into his gooey filling, and Barron doesn't suit the man he's becoming.

I still want to know about Jaxx calling him Bastian. Obvi

that's a takeoff from his real given name, but I'm sure there's a personal story behind calling him that.

The next half an hour is spent with the five of us filling our faces and them updating me on what I missed.

"So, when Hawk's soul crystal triggered, we finally had a direction," Jaxx says, snatching the last onion ring from the cardboard container. "Lukas had the pilot hover over the ledge and he dropped a harness down. Once Hawk got you tethered, we pulled you up and into the helicopter."

"Man, are you kidding me? I've been trying to get you to tie me up all along and you choose the moment when I'm unconscious?"

Hawk rolls his eyes and his head drops forward.

"Too soon?"

"Yeah," he whispers. "Too soon."

Okay, so Hawk is still feeling the aftershocks of the ordeal. I'll have to address that privately in a bit. "And where are we now?"

"Don't you recognize this room?" Kotah raises his hand and I give our surroundings my full attention The moment I clue in, I'm filled with a flood of warm and fuzzy. "The Bronco Room. We're in our suite."

Hawk snorts. "Adjoining rooms you can rent by the hour with a shared bathroom is hardly a suite. I wanted to take you somewhere appropriate, but was outvoted."

I smile. "I'm with them on this one, sorry. Did we get the Stud Room too?"

"You better believe it, beautiful." Brant sits on the end of the bed and reaches for an abandoned bag of burgers. "Was there any doubt? It's like this place was made for us."

Hawk rolls his eyes. "In what realm does this place speak to who we are?"

I giggle at his frustration. "When we were here the first time, you ran away and hid instead of having fun with us. This is your chance for a mulligan. Let us show you the charm of The Rusty Spur."

"I don't need a mulligan. We're here because this place was close, Lukas already knew the security, and I thought it would boost morale to regroup in a place you enjoyed."

"And it's close to the palace and the Portal Gate," I add. "So that's handy. Is that where you think my phoenix was heading when she flew off on her own?"

Hawk grabs up the discarded wrappers of almost twenty eaten burgers. "Yeah. I think it's your phoenix's instinct to go to the Portal Gate now that our mating bond is complete and all four pieces of your pendant have been retrieved."

"How do we make them into my pendant?"

They all shrug, looking blank.

Hawk tosses the garbage into the bin at the door and boomerangs back. "I'm sure the universe magic will take care of that when the time comes."

"That's how things have been workin' so far," Jaxx says.

"Now that we're officially ready to kick ass," Brant says. "We can get this party rocking."

"We're not totally ready," I say, holding up my finger. "If you remember, I still fall on my face when I land."

Hawk shakes his head. "The last few times you've landed, you've been fine. I think your wildling side knows exactly what she needs to do. Your human side just needs to give her the reins to do it."

"I'll take your word for it." I flop back onto the pillows. "Jaxx, will you take this poker out of my arm, please? I need to pee. And now that I'm awake, eating, and drinking, I should be good to go, right?"

I extend my wrist toward Jaxx and wince as he eases the intervenous line out of my vein.

Instead of a bandage to cover the puncture hole, Jaxx brings my wrist to my mouth. "Lick it."

"*Annnd* that's the title of your sex tape," Brant says.

Jaxx laughs. "Yes it is, but also, I want to see if her saliva will seal the wound."

I do as he suggests and swipe my tongue over the needle hole, then swing my feet out from the covers. "And, do I by chance have clothes to wear?"

Hawk picks up my duffle from the floor and sets it on the end of the bed. "We'll give you a moment to freshen up and can meet you downstairs."

Brant chuffs. "Speak for yourself, Hawk. What if our wildling sides don't want to be dismissed? I, for one, need to take a minute with my mate. If she's well and willing, there are matters which need to be addressed before we consider her getting dressed."

Hawk pegs him with a droll stare and frowns. "We're all feeling the pull of needing to claim our mate, Bear. But we are as much men as we are animals. The five of us going at it when the world's closing in is not wise."

The growl of Brant's bear holds all the challenge and frustration my poor bear can muster against an alpha. "Sending my bear out into the world when I can barely contain the rage of nearly losing her is not wise. I'm warning you, Hawk, blood will be shed."

I raise my hands. "It's okay, guys. We'll make time for reassuring your wild sides and then get straight back to it. We'll save the all-night marathon for later, but surely we can take the edge off. Let me pee. Brant, sweetie, I'm well and willing, don't you worry."

CHAPTER TWENTY

Hawk

$\mathcal{I}$ follow Calli down the little hallway that connects the two rooms I rented and when she turns right and closes herself into the bathroom, I continue straight ahead into the Stud room. With all the control I have left, I ease the door shut with a soft *click* and shake out my trembling hands. It kills me that we honestly didn't know if she would come back to us.

I barely make it to the bed before my legs give out and I'm ass-planting on the mattress. Bending forward, I drop my head into my hands and try to get control of my shakes.

It doesn't do any of them any good to see me losing my shit, but yeah... consider it lost.

"Hey, hotness." Jaxx closes himself in with me during my moment of pansy-assed-pussy-whipped meltdown. "Any chance you need one of my famous Stanton hugs? Bound to cure whatever ails you."

I let off a sob and open my arms. He drops to the carpet between my feet and wraps his arms around me. The reality of the past twenty-four hours takes me. Following Calli further and further from our mates, getting shot…

"I couldn't save her, Jaxx. We were stranded on that fucking ledge and there wasn't a damned thing my money, or influence, or alpha autocratic bullshit could do to keep her from dying."

Jaxx tightens his hold and I'd swear he's the only thing holding me together. Without his crushing embrace, I'd shatter into a million tiny pieces and blow away on the wind. "It was way too close. No argument. Still, it's our win. She's recovering and with her healing ability, she'll be full-strength in another hour or two."

"Fuck. I never imagined she'd go down so hard so fast."

Jaxx eases back and cradles my face in his palms. "So, now we know. After her phoenix battles, we carb-load her and keep her system runnin' smooth. From what you described, she flew all night, had just woken up and had to battle, and then flew a great distance again. It was too much."

"Too much for me, too."

He leans forward and brushes his lips over mine. "You'd never know it. From the outside lookin' in, you handled everythin' with the same strength and proficiency as always."

"Okay, now you're shining me on. You don't have to flatter me, you know. I'm a sure thing."

Jaxx chuckles and kisses me again. My jaguar's kisses carry tons of emotion and subtext. Over the past weeks, it's been my pleasure to learn to speak his love language. With this kiss, he's reassuring me that he's here for me and that when I'm shaky, he'll always step in to support me.

I absorb all the love and strength he offers and draw a deep, steadying breath. "Thank you."

Jaxx winks, his stunning turquoise eyes dancing with emotion. "I'd say anytime but I'd rather not repeat this one."

"You and me both." I cup his jaw with my palm and pull him

back to my lips for one more kiss. "I love you hard, Jaguar. Hydrogen."

"Hydrogen, Bastian. Right back attcha."

With that, my world rights itself once more and I give him the nod. "Okay, let's settle our animals, and then we'll be ready to tackle the next disaster."

"That's the spirit," Jaxx says. "Some might think pessimistic, but those of us in the know recognize realism when we hear it. The next disaster awaits right around the corner conspiring to bash us in the balls."

I bark a laugh, so fucking thankful for Jaxx. "That should be on a Hallmark card."

When the two of us exit the Stud Room, we pass Kotah in the shower and find Calli and Brant in the throes of easing the bear's anxiety. For all the strength of the man and beast, the gentle reverence he uses when making love to her always surprises me.

My body's reaction to the scene in front of me is immediate and undeniable. Yeah, I need her too—hell, I'd bet my entire fortune that I need her more. I don't deny they were all scared but there's no way their panic could compare to what I went through.

I peel off my clothes and toss them over the chair.

Jaxx does the same and climbs onto the bed. I marvel at how comfortable the jaguar is with Calli, Brant, and Kotah. Yes, he was the first one to mate and has spent the most time in the most situations with them, but I think it speaks a lot to the man as well. Jaxx is simply a warm and amazing lover.

Hanging back a bit, I give Brant his moment.

I wasn't trying to cock-block the guy when I said we should move on, I just thought we should stay on task.

I see his point though, if my hawk got out of control someone might get hacked up with my talons or torn by my beak. There's no walking away from the kind of damage Brant's bear would do if he lost his hold.

It must be a weight on him to know if he's not in control at all times the people around him will end up dead. Maybe that's why he deflects and cracks wise all the time. Or maybe that's from the scars of not remembering his parents.

Oh, to be lucky enough not to remember my father.

I'd never want to forget my mother... but yeah, I'd lose my father in an instant.

Even to know the man is nearby practically liquifies my bowels. I don't want him anywhere near me... or my mates.

"We okay, avian?" I blink out of my musings and focus on the worry in Brant's eyes. "You look upset. If it's me or what I said earlier—"

I stand, grip the hair at the back of his neck, and pull him in for a kiss. His hands are warm on my bare hips and he meets me chest-to-chest. When I ease back, I nip his bottom lip and smile. "It's not you that upset me. We're good."

Brant nods. "Okay, good. I tend to wear thin on people. I'm trying here, but if I fuck up, know that I don't intend to piss you off... unless I'm trying to piss you off."

I kiss him again and then smack his bare ass. "You didn't fuck up. Go get cleaned up. There's still lots of daylight ahead of us and I want to get to the sex marathon part Calli mentioned as soon as possible, don't you?"

His cocky smile returns and my anxiety eases. "You know I do."

Brant jogs off toward the bathroom hall and I watch as Jaxx's body arches and his eyes roll closed. The two of them are joined and he rolls them on their sides, his leg lazily hanging over her hip.

Climbing on the bed, I slide in behind Calli and reach across over her arm to caress Jaxx's ribs. The jaguar eases out of her pussy and I kiss her neck. "Are you good, Spitfire? I don't have to bed you. I'm content to hold you and not be the fourth."

"Shit," Jaxx says, his smile fading. "I didn't even think of that. I should've opted out. You were put through the most and likely need the reassurance more than any of us. Sorry."

I kiss Calli's shoulder and nuzzle into her neck. "Doesn't matter. Nothing matters except Calli thriving. Everything else is white noise."

Calli wriggles her butt against my pelvis and I close my eyes and groan. "You're hard, aren't you?"

"I couldn't lay next to you and not be, my love."

"Then don't waste it. Isn't the saying use it or lose it?"

I chuckle. "Only if you're sure."

She rolls to face me and her gaze is so knowing I swear she can see directly into my soul. "You need me and your hawk needs me. I'm right here and I need you too. I hated seeing you shot. I feel your pain. I'm here for you."

Shifting forward, I bring her knee onto my hip and press my hand flat on her lower back bringing us together. Her core is wet and welcoming and my eyes roll back in my head as I sink into her heat.

"I love you." My voice comes out as barely more than a whisper, but I know she hears me. Calli always hears me.

"I love you back."

"And thank the universe for that." Wrapping my arms around her, we move in slow tandem, my hawk content for the first time in more than twenty-four long, stressful hours.

Jaxx eases Calli onto her back and I roll with her to mount her missionary. Who knew I could derive so much pleasure from the simple act of vanilla sex with my mates.

Jaxx runs a gentle caress from my shoulder, down my back, and over the rounds of my ass. His touch is kind and giving. He's not looking for anything in return.

He's simply loving me.

I clutch his hand and kiss Calli with all the relief I feel that she's well and mine to love. Our bodies joined. Our connection firm. Our touches gentle. Her legs wrap around my thighs and she holds me tight.

I come in a surge of emotion, my release not the hot explosion I'm used to but a cresting wave of pleasure pushing out of me with a primal rightness.

I've never experienced anything like it before.

"I don't want to overanalyze, but I honestly think this is the first time I've ever truly made love to anyone before."

Calli's smile sears my heart. "There he is."

I chuckle and kiss her nose. "There who is?"

"You told me there isn't a gentler, romantic version of a man inside you waiting to be coaxed out. You said you are acerbic and cruel and nothing more. And yet, here we are."

"Yep," Kotah says, climbing onto the bed with us. He kisses my shoulder and flops down beside us. "Here we are a fully bonded quint."

Brant's chuckle rumbles from the side of the bed. "And though it doesn't happen often, I get to say you were wrong, Hawk. You are so much more than you thought—much more than what I thought too."

I try to stay in the moment, but honestly, I can't keep a straight face. Laughter bubbles up and I shake my head. "Are we seriously having a heart-to-heart when I've got my cock plugged in Calli?"

Kotah laughs. "All hail the sacred wand of truth."

Okay, that busts everyone up.

I kiss Calli's cheek, wink at Jaxx, and retreat to the bathroom to clean up and let things settle into place. It still seems unreal that those four are my mates and they love me.

But it's real.

Calli

After a quick shower, I head into the bedroom, grab my duffle off the floor, and unzip things. "What did you boys bring me to wear?" I pull out a pair of jaguar print undies and matching bra and giggle. "I take it, this is from you, puss?"

Jaxx's grin splits wide. "*Moi?* What makes you say that?"

I bend over, hook my feet into the leg holes, and pull the sexy, silky gitch up over my hips. "How far are we from the Portal Gate? Any chance we can get there and get things taken care of today?"

Hawk shrugs. "I sent Lukas to check in with the scout team and secure the area for our arrival. Knowing my father, he won't stop trying to thwart us until he knows for certain the five of us are dead and no one is going to open the gate."

I wince. "Do you think he'd have you killed?"

He laughs. "Oh, baby, he'd pull the trigger himself and smile while doing it."

I finish getting dressed and zip up my duffle. "Are we leaving and going on or leaving and coming back?"

"Better to err on the side of having our stuff with us."

I hand my stuff off to Brant to take. "My thinking exactly. Let me do a final room check."

The five of us head down the saloon steps and I head over to the bar to thank Clara for her hospitality once again. "You look a damned sight better than you did when they carried you in here last night, girlfriend. There were a lot of worried men bustling around up there."

I nod. "Yeah, I got caught out in the wild without warm clothes or food and drink. I don't suggest it. It sucked bad."

"The most important thing is that you're steady and ready to roll now," Jaxx says.

"And you bounced back fast," Clara says.

Jaxx nods. "She amazes us. Every. Single. Day."

The *thwump-thwump-thwump* of chopper blades cutting through the air outside brings our attention to the return of Lukas with the intel we'll need for the next chapter of our adventure.

"Thanks again, Clara. See you soon."

"See ye, girlfriend."

Hawk, Kotah, and Brant are waiting at the edge of the property staring out at the farmer's field behind the Rusty Spur. When the twin-engine, Eurocopter AS365 Dauphin settles on the ground, Lukas jumps out and jogs over.

By the look on his face, our bad day is about to go into the crapper. I expect him to rip the bandage off and get straight to it. He doesn't. He takes a beat, smiles at me, and dips his chin. "I'm glad to see you up and about. How are you feeling?"

"Much better, thank you."

Then, he looks toward Hawk and the others and his smile drains away. "I've got bad news and worse news. Which would you like first?"

Hawk grimaces and throws up his hands. "Let's go with the bad news."

He nods and turns to Kotah. "I'm sorry, Wolf. Your sister called me a half-hour ago. Your father passed. You've been called in to begin your reign as Fae Prime."

"*Fuck*," Hawk says.

I move in for a hug and Jaxx, Brant, and Hawk all pile on. "I'm sorry, sweetie."

"Me too, Wolf," Hawk says, pulling us tight to my chest. "I'll move mountains to make this bearable for you, I swear."

Kotah looks numb. He squeezes my hand in his and nods. "It's not like we weren't prepared, right? We knew it was coming. When do I have to go back to the palace?"

"I told your sister we'd be there as soon as possible."

Hawk scrubs a rough hand over his face and sighs. "Okay, if

that's only the bad news, I can't fucking wait to hear the worse news."

Lukas's expression oozes with a look of hopeless apology and we all brace for impact. "Either your father or the corrupt members of the council, or some other dickhole with a hefty supply of C4 explosive got to the Portal Gate this morning. Our team is dead and the gate is gone."

I gasp, nausea rolling and twisting in the pit of my belly.

Hawk steps away, throwing his fists through the air and letting off a stream of curses that are not only colorful but anatomically impossible.

Jaxx winces and moves in closer. "Any chance the connection between the realms could've survived without the gate?"

Lukas shakes his head. "No. The whole area is blown to smithereens. Nothing but rubble and pebbles left."

"Fan-fucking-tastic," Brant says, kicking a chunk of dirt at the vacant field.

"We took too long," I say, the pain of defeat stinging my eyes. "This is my fault. I should've worked harder and developed faster. I failed everyone. I'm so sorry."

Jaxx shakes his head and hugs me as the rest of them wave that off.

"That's bullshit, Spitfire. You went from dead human to fully-bonded, completely developed phoenix in under two months. That's incredible. No one could've done it better."

"Barron's right," Lukas says. "Our mistake was in not anticipating the enemy better. The Black Knight was ahead of us every step of the way. We were defensive and never got a chance to be offensive."

"The thought that my father won again burns my balls."

My poor avian. It sucks when you can't get ahead of your past no matter how hard you try. I understand that frustration. "Do we have men at the site now?"

Lukas nods. "We're collecting our dead and sorting through

the damage. Whoever destroyed it did a thorough job and left it abandoned. The site is secure."

"Alright then, that's our first stop. Then we'll continue to the palace to get Kotah sorted out with his Fae Prime obligations. I want everyone's thinking caps on. The universe didn't pick us at random. We need to figure out our next steps. There's no way Hawk's father wins this. No. Fucking. Way."

The five of us get into the helicopter and buckle up.

As much as I hate Kotah going through the motions on this whole Fae Prime thing, part of me is glad to head back to our suite. With the amount of travel and jostling around we've done from south to north to west to east, there's something to be said for our home away from home.

"Are you okay, my prince?"

Kotah nods. "I am. I think, in many ways, my father died for me a long time ago. The man he's been for the past decade represents all the pain and judgment I faced. In a way, it's kind of a relief to know that's over. Does that sound awful?"

Brant grunts and when he shakes his head, his loose brown curls swing against his shoulders. "It sounds honest, Wolf. And no matter what faces you need to put on for the rest of the realm, with us, you can always be honest."

Jaxx shifts to sit on the edge of the bench across from us and clasps his wrist. "We're with you. It'll serve them all right if you kick down their sandcastles and build your own world from the ground up."

I swivel my chair and take his other hand. "I meant what I said. The universe didn't pick the five of us at random."

"What do you mean, *Chigua?*"

"I mean, Jaxx recognized who and what I was from the first moment I transitioned and has been our foundation from the get-go. Brant knew about the missing kids and the corruption within FCO. Hawk has the resources and the political know-how to walk into any situation and get shit done. And you just became the most powerful individual fae on this side of the two realms. No way that's a coincidence."

Kotah assesses that and seems to agree.

"And you, beautiful?" Brant asks. "Where do you put yourself in the universe's plans?"

"The more I think about it, the more I think Riley does come from some kind of precognition species of fae and knew who I was destined to become. I believe every scrape she got me out of and every lesson she forced me to learn readied me for you four and my task as the phoenix."

"Which kinda sucks now that the Portal Gate's been destroyed."

I hold up a finger. "The primary gate is destroyed, but when Jaxx explained to me about how the gates were dismantled to ensure containment of the civil war in StoneHaven, he said at one time there were many gates."

"Were, kitten. I also said they were destroyed."

"Destroyed, dismantled, or decommissioned?"

Hawk leans back on the bench and rubs the nape of his neck. "I like where you're going with this, Spitfire, but that's a fine distinction. Yeah, maybe the Kansas gate was made primary because of its location in the center of the country but there were many gates at one point."

Jaxx straightens. "Do you honestly think there might be another gate somewhere that we could reactivate and use to open the link to the other realm?"

I shrug. "It's possible, isn't it?"

Hawk nods. "And at this point, it's our best shot. We'll have to move fast and hard to get ahead of my father on this, but yeah, let's work that angle."

When the helicopter lands at the former site of the Portal Gate we all get out to assess the rubble. The place looks like a warzone. When the hum of the rotors quiets, Lukas excuses the men on Hawk's team and escorts the five of us to what—until recently—was the entire point of my destiny.

"Shit," Jaxx says, looking ill. "It seems anti-climactic to be here like this now, don't you think?"

I toe the rocks and rubble feeling the wrongness of what happened here. Hawk lost a team of eight men. That will hurt him deeply. He'll think it's his fault because his father is behind it. My poor avian.

I squat down and press both of my hands against the pitted ground. The energy that tingles up my arms and into the core of my chest speaks to me on a level I don't understand. "We need to have this cleaned up and restore what we can. The magic of this place is hurting."

"Hurting, beautiful?" Brant says, canting his head.

"It's hard to explain." I brush the bits of rock and rubble from my palms. "Lukas? Do you know any magic spells that will release negative intentions and allow nature to heal?"

Lukas shrugs. "There are dozens of cleansing rituals that can be performed. Why? What exactly do you feel?"

"I'm not sure. It might sound weird but somehow I know that the magic here isn't gone... it's injured. Whoever destroyed the gate thought it was all about the gate, but there's more to this place than that. The site needs some TLC."

He shrugs. "Okay, once you're all settled back at the palace, I'll come back and see what I can do. You might have to come back with me because I'm not tuned in to the same frequency you are. I don't feel any of that."

As his words fill the air, I felt the rightness of that. "Done deal. In the meantime, how do we get a list of all the former gate locations?"

"Mama would know that better than anyone," Jaxx says.

"Did Mama and Jonathan return to the palace with Doc and Keyla when they heard about the passing of the Prime?"

Lukas nods. "They did."

"Then that's where we need to be." Kotah draws a steadying breath and lifts his chin. "Calli's right. I'm the fucking Fae Prime. It's time I start acting the part. Hawk, you and I need to sit down and pull apart what's working and what's not. Jaxx is right, it's time to stomp on sandcastles."

"That's the spirit, Wolf," Brant says.

Jaxx's grin is far too sexy. "And didn't someone mention a sex marathon later?"

Lukas puts his hands over his ears and heads back toward the helicopter. "Lalalalala."

Hawk gestures for us to follow and I feel the pull of the fae magic. This site isn't finished with us. Not by a long shot. "Spitfire? Are you ready?"

I nod... and for the first time since this all began I can answer that with confidence. "Yeah, I am ready."

~~ THE END ~~

AFTERWORD

Thank you for reading Hawk's Heart. I hope you enjoyed getting to know the quint better as they align and ready for what is to come. Don't miss the final installment. Claim book 5 – Jaguar's Passion now.

If you are inclined to help a girl out, it would be amazing if you could leave a star rating or review
If you want more, join my newsletter and be notified when new books launch and for all my news and sales!

ABOUT THE AUTHOR

Author Notes
Written on 09/20/2020

Thank you so much for reading, and since you're reading this—for continuing to read.

In these crazy times of stress and division, opinions and judgement, I love the escape of spending time with Calli, Jaxx, Hawk, Kotah, and Brant.

Like all my books, their journey is about finding where you belong and who you belong with. Whether that's one person in a traditional monogamous relationship or five in a polyamorous one. Live and let live.

Book five in the series—Jaguar's Passion—will seal the deal on the quint as they work to open the portal between two worlds and fulfill their destiny.

I hope you'll come along for the ride.

Then, after Jaguar's Passion, the series will continue with the building of another harem in the same world and with the same cast. Stay tuned for that.

Wishing you all lives filled with laughter and love.

Hugs to all,

JL

Find Me

My Direct Sales Site: Shopify

My books

Web page – www.jlmadore.com

Email – jlmadorewrites@gmail.com

Newsletter – JL Series Updates

ALSO BY

Book 1 – Captured by the Magi

Book 2 – Jesse and the Magi Vault

Book 3 – The Makings of a Magi Knight

Book 4 – Clash with the Magi Council

Book 5 – The Unstoppable Storme

Club Sanguine

Book 1 – Moonstone Maelstrom

Book 2 - Sunstone Sacrifice

JL's More Traditional M/F, M/M, or Menage

The Watchers of the Gray Series (Paranormal)

Book 1 – Watcher Untethered – Zander

Book 2 – Watcher Redeemed – Kyrian

Book 3 – Watcher Reborn – Danel

Book 4 – Watcher Divided – Phoenix

Book 5 – Watcher United – Seth

Book 6 – Watcher Compelled – Bo

Book 7 – Watcher Unfeigned – Brennus

Book 8 – Watcher Exposed – Taharqa

The Scourge Survivor Series (Fantasy)

Book 1 – Blaze Ignites

Book 2 – Ursa Unearthed

Book 3 – Torrent of Tears

Book 4 – Blind Spirit

Book 5 – Fate's Journey

Book 6 – Savage Love – epilogue novella

Aliens of Atlantis Series (Sci-Fi)

Book 1 – Taryn's Tiderider

Book 2 – Kai's Captive

Book 3 – Alyandra's Shadow